Traitor's end

'I am his death. He must kill me. Even now he is thinking it is too late.' But is he to be believed, the eccentric, ageing French expatriate who bursts into Chief Superintendent Gently's flat one October afternoon? He implores protection. He has seen a man whom he recognizes as a Resistance traitor, and whom he alone can identify – and who has also recognized him! 'Monsieur, I am in danger. In deadly danger!' But . . . after forty or more years? Gently soothes him down, dismisses him, and promptly forgets him in the great wind storm that follows.

But, when the storm casualties are counted the next day, one is the tourist named by the Frenchman. Pierre Bernay had been camping in Sussex, where his caravette had been crushed under a giant beach tree.

Only . . . was he alive when the van was crushed? The injuries are suspicious, and Gently discovers that, in Bernay's home town, he is regarded not as a traitor but as a Resistance hero. Meanwhile Bernay's widow arrives, calling for vengeance, to be followed by agents yet more sinister. The hunt is up! And Jean Caudry, the informant, flees his shop in the quiet Sussex town.

Bernay or Caudry – which was the traitor? And what can be the end of this grim affair? It sits on the conscience of Gently's French wife, who feels wretchedly involved in the business, and who, at last, may have to decide what shall be the fate of a traitor to France. After forty odd years do you execute him, or merely spit in his face?

Alan Hunter's thirty-sixth Chief Superintendent Gently murder mystery has all the deftly professional qualities which his many thousands of devotees have come to expect and receive.

Other murder cases investigated
by Chief Superintendent Gently, CID.

TRAITOR'S END

Alan Hunter

Constable London

First published in Great Britain 1988
by Constable & Company Ltd
10 Orange Street, London WC2H 7EG
Copyright © by Alan Hunter 1988
Set in Palatino 10pt by
Selectmove Ltd, London
Printed in Great Britain by
St Edmundsbury Press Ltd
Bury St Edmunds, Suffolk

British Library CIP data
Hunter, Alan, *1922*–
Traitors end
I. Title
823'.914[F]

ISBN 0 09 468690 4

The characters and events in this book are
fictitious; the locale is sketched from life.

1

Intuition? Déjà-vu? – Freud would have none of these. Yet something I felt, a sort of sadness, as I turned into Lime Walk that afternoon. There was no reason for it. Business was slack, I had left Dutt in charge and quit early. It was a Thursday, the week-end beckoned, and the grape-vine suggested no tumults on the morrow. So I was in good spirits when I caught the tube, when I walked up Kensington Church Street; and in fact I had only just reached Lime Walk when a glow of hazed sunlight suddenly lit it. This, after rain had threatened all day: the familiar street awakening with colour: the double row of limes, still hung with yellow leaf, the rococo terraces, glimpse of Holland Park: a moment of magic. And yet? Perhaps the mood of autumn, of summer gone? Somehow, it seemed more poignant than that, more solemn, and as though . . .? I didn't know.

On Thursdays Gabrielle visited friends so I was returning to an empty flat. I went through to the kitchen and brewed some coffee, still with that odd feeling upon me. The first stages of a cold? Dutt had been sneezing. But I rarely picked up an infection. No: it was psychic, not physical: something evoked by that moment of sun. The sun, the trees. Which soon would be bare. Probably nothing more than that. Well, now the sun had gone as quickly as it had come, and the long-delayed rain begun to smear the pavements.

I took my coffee through to the lounge and set it down

while I filled my pipe. But I hadn't yet got a match to it when the Frenchman came banging on my door.

A squeal of tyres had heralded his arrival, and the battering at the door followed straight after – presumably he hadn't found the bell-push, or his exigency precluded such niceties.

'Monsieur, monsieur!'

'All right – I'm coming!'

'Monsieur, I am being followed!'

As I opened the door he thrust it wide and came plunging into the hall.

'What the devil –!'

'I am being followed. I am being followed by an assassin!'

'There is no one following you.'

'A man, monsieur. He is driving a blue-and-white car-avette.'

'There is no blue-and-white caravette.'

'In a moment, he will be here!'

But just then not a single vehicle was perambulating the cul-de-sac of Lime Walk.

'Control yourself, monsieur.'

'Please close the door!'

'There is no need for such behaviour.'

'Oh monsieur, you do not understand –'

'Then perhaps you will be kind enough to explain.'

'But monsieur, close the door!'

I did close the door, though not without another glance at the empty street. The fellow was shaking, his eyes staring. He placed his hands together as though in prayer.

'Oh monsieur, Monsieur Jont-Lee –'

'The name is Gently. And who are you?'

'A poor Frenchman, monsieur, who lives in this country, and who has heard of your fame, your exploits –'

'Who gave you this address?'

'Monsieur, the phone-book.'

High time we went ex-directory!

8

'And now you come rushing here, tailed by an assassin?'

'Monsieur, I am in danger. In deadly danger!'

I looked him over, this trembling visitor. He was a man aged in his middle sixties, tall, lean, a hatchet profile, features withered and pale. Short grey hair. The staring eyes a pale grey-blue. Long arms, large, lank hands. Dressed in a slightly shabby lounge suit with a spotted bow-tie, also shabby.

'What's your name?'

'Jean Caudry, monsieur.'

'And you say you are a resident here?'

'For more than forty years, monsieur. I am a poor shopkeeper, a widower.'

'And who would wish to assassinate a poor shopkeeper?'

'Monsieur, if I could but sit down – '

I stared at him, shrugged, pointed the way into the lounge. He ambled in, stared fearfully at the window, then sought a chair in a corner distant from it. My coffee was waiting. I drank some. I lit my pipe. I sat.

'Now.'

'I am a poor shopkeeper – '

'That point has been sufficiently made!'

'Monsieur, you do not understand, it is because of my shop that I encounter this man. It is the afternoon of yesterday when a blue-and-white caravette parks outside. It is on double yellow lines, no matter, in our town the police have great understanding, and this man enters with an empty gas cylinder which he is wishing to exchange. I am then engaged with two customers who are buying cagoules and so, at first, pay this man no attention.'

'And where is this happening?'

'At Leyhurst, monsieur.'

'Leyhurst!'

'A small town some kilometres from Brighton.'

'I am aware of the situation of Leyhurst, monsieur, but not why its problems should land on my doorstep.'

'Because, monsieur, you are my last hope!'

'I think I have heard enough,' I said. 'If you really are in trouble, Caudry, the people to go to are your congenial policemen at Leyhurst.'

'But, monsieur, monsieur – '

'That's all,' I said.

He was wriggling his long body like an eel.

'Monsieur, I must tell you I have been to our policemen, and my story they do not believe. It is so long ago, you understand, and of what happened in France they know nothing. But you, monsieur, who have a French wife, and perhaps an acquaintance with my countrymen, you will believe me. Because if you do not, poor Jean Caudry is a dead duck.'

I gazed at him long. I could well believe the attitude of the Leyhurst Police; he had about him something fey, almost of being mentally deficient. But he was scarcely that. Behind those grey eyes a keen intelligence was working. He could see me wavering, and over his withered features flickered an ingratiating smirk. But it vanished quickly.

'So I'm listening,' I said. 'But don't think that will help you, Caudry. If I suspect there is anything in what you tell me, I shall still refer it back to Leyhurst.'

'Monsieur, what I tell is the truth.'

'Then cut it short. Who is wanting to kill you?'

He glanced furtively at the window. 'Pierre Bernay. He was the man who came into my shop.'

'Pierre Bernay?'

'Who is known to me, monsieur, as the betrayer of the comrades of Trouville.'

And probably I should have thrown him out then, with a homily about wasting police time. Because, ever since the war, and more particularly in the neighbourhood of the Channel ports, rumours about the French Resistance have been going their stubborn rounds. They have been quoted in excuse of smuggling, burglary and grievous

10

bodily harm, but never yet, to my knowledge, have been shown to have any foundation. Of late years the incidence has fallen, doubtless as memories of the war fade; but here, complete with horns and tail, the legend was erupting in Lime Walk, and sponsored by an absurd character with the aspect of a Monsieur Hulot. All this went through my mind. And yet I didn't throw him out. I didn't, because I'd caught the look in his eyes as he spoke those words. Momentary, gone in a flash, a hard, thrusting, feline stare: a stare that chilled: that delivered a shock. And I didn't throw him out. Instead, I repeated:

'Pierre Bernay?'

'You will not have heard of him, monsieur. No one has heard of him. I, I alone know him to be the guilty man.'

'And after forty years you recognise him?'

'But yes, who can forget that face? He has a small beard now, is grey, is lined, his age perhaps nearing seventy. But the same man. Our eyes meet just once as he takes the gas cylinder, pays the money. But I know him, monsieur, and, alack, he knows me.'

'You were both members of the Resistance?'

'I was, you may say, on the fringe, monsieur. A young man who possessed a bicycle and was agreeable to run their errands. I am not in their counsels, in their activities, just a young fool who is useful. Nevertheless I would have been shot if *les Chleuhs* had got their hands on me.'

'The which?'

'The Germans, monsieur. It was a name we used which they would not understand. Perhaps in a bar, yes? When we are drinking, and there are Germans at the next table. Then we talk about *les Chleuhs*, and they do not know who it is we curse.'

'And this was at Trouville?'

'But yes. Trouville.'

'Where Pierre Bernay was an active member?'

'He was our wireless-operator, monsieur, and remained so until the end. We are the lucky ones, people say. All

11

around us groups are being arrested, tortured, shot. But not at Trouville. Never at Trouville. For us, *les Chleuhs* have the blind spot. Is it because our security is so excellent? Monsieur, I will leave you to judge.'

'You had a traitor.'

'Pierre Bernay.'

'What makes you certain it was he?'

'Oh monsieur, monsieur! In the end comes D-Day, and that same day the luck runs out. *Les Chleuhs* have no more use for us, heh? Now we become a liability. So then the roundings-up, the shootings. Every man but one. Pierre Bernay.'

'Also presumably yourself.'

'I had been despatched with a message, monsieur. I return to hear the shootings going on and am able to make my escape from Trouville. I dare not go home. I make my way to Rouen, where I am taken in one of their sweeps. By chance, they have not learned of my connection with the comrades, and I am sent to a labour camp in the Ruhr.'

'Then you don't know for certain that Bernay was the man.'

'He is alive. All the others were shot.'

'The same might be said of yourself, monsieur.'

'But, monsieur, he was with the others, and I was not. At that time he is ceaselessly with the wireless, which is in the cellar where they meet. It is there that they were surrounded, and in the courtyard without where they were shot. Only, Bernay was not shot. Because yesterday he is buying gas in my shop.'

'But all the others were shot?'

'*Oui*, yes.'

'So how do you know that?'

He writhed.

'Monsieur, to the labour camp is brought this man from Trouville, and he is able to tell me all. Why should I lie? Every member of our group was executed. Except Bernay.'

'He, like yourself, may have chanced to escape.'

12

'Never. Unless *les Chleuhs* permitted it.'

'In that case, wouldn't others have suspected him?'

'Then he has killed them, monsieur. As he means to kill me.'

I drank up my coffee; I wasn't persuaded. There were too many holes in this story. Also, given that it was true, what need would Bernay have to fear such testimony now? Clearly his innocence had long been accepted: in France, no suspicion attached to his name. The evidence was circumstantial and in part hearsay, and all this had happened above forty years since. Caudry was watching me. I said:

'Monsieur, you tell me a very strange story! That you are in fear is plain, but can we be so sure that you recognised the man?'

'Believe me, monsieur!'

'Yet you saw him for how long?'

'Upon that occasion, a few minutes.'

'On that occasion?'

'He comes again. Monsieur, he was parked near my shop this morning. I am serving a customer, I go to the window to fetch some mittens from a display. And there I see him, eyeing the shop, with his van parked a few yards away. He strolls up and down. He watches. He lights a cigarette, and spits towards me. I am in a state of nerves so great that I can scarcely make change for the customer. It is after this that I close my shop, and, in desperation, come to you.'

'With this man trailing you?'

His eyes slewed to the window.

'In my mirror, I saw the van following. It was there as I drove through the town. It was there when the town was left behind. I drove faster. So too did the van. I turned suddenly into a byroad, drove fast, made other turns, returned again to the main road. Then I had lost him, but for how long? Monsieur, such a van was behind me in traffic near here. You will say it was perhaps a similar van, but, monsieur, I know the man I deal with.'

13

'But what danger do you represent to him, Caudry, when it would be only your word against his?'

'Do you not see? But one word, if I breathe it, will set the comrades on his trail.'

'The Resistance – still?'

'But yes, monsieur. The Resistance still. It does not die. The traitor of Trouville is still to be found, hunted down, brought to justice. And I, I alone, know his name – and he, he knows that I know it. I am his death. He must kill me. Even now he is thinking it may be too late.'

'He is perhaps an innocent French tourist who has startled you by a resemblance.'

'No monsieur, no. I implore that you believe me. I must have protection, and have it now.'

'Monsieur, I have had this street under observation since you entered my house. From this window I can see in either direction. And no blue-and-white van has appeared.'

'It is but that he waits for me elsewhere.'

'Or that you have been mistaken all along.'

'Oh, monsieur! And I thought you would understand me.'

'You must admit it's an odd story.'

He did his silly writhing act, and accompanied it with a stare of reproach. Just something about him I wasn't swallowing, and it wasn't merely the theatricality. I was remembering that stare of earlier: its sudden, violent penetration. It didn't go with the rest; and I couldn't forget it. It was stopping any sympathy I might have felt for him. I said:

'Monsieur, you will remain here while I consult on the telephone with my colleagues.'

'I shall have protection, monsieur?'

'That we shall see.'

'Monsieur, my life is in your hands!'

I grunted, rose, went through to the hall; closed the door of the lounge behind me. Directory connected me with Leyhurst, who put me through to a Detective Chief Inspector Ringmer. Compliments exchanged, I said:

'What do we know of a Leyhurst shopkeeper called Jean Caudry?'

'Oh lor'!' Ringmer said. 'Don't tell me he's been up there bugging the Yard.'

'He came to me personally.'

'I'm sorry about that, sir. Just give him the bum's rush, that's my advice. I'll have a word with him when he gets back here. We can't have our nutters breaking out like this.'

'You would describe him as a nutter?'

'Solid fruit-cake, sir. He's pretty well-known round this manor. To hear him tell the tale you'd think he ran the French Resistance single-handed.'

'He says he took his story to you.'

'Yes sir. And I told him what he could do with it. It wasn't the first time, sir. Here in Leyhurst we see a lot of French tourists, and Moossoo Caudry would have us believe that the best part of them are Resistance villains. I'd say he had a guilty conscience. But he's never given us any real trouble.'

'He has naturalisation, of course?'

'Yes sir. All legal. He came over after the war with an army maintenance unit, who had taken him on as a civvy storekeeper. Then he got a job here at The Camping Shop and married the owner's daughter. Now he's a widower, living alone in a flat over the shop. Does all right there too – I buy my own equipment from Moossoo.'

'Has he ever asked for protection before?'

'No sir. This is a new one.'

'You wouldn't have seen this fellow he talks about?'

'In the blue-and-white van, sir? I saw him only a moment ago. The van went past here, heading towards Seldon. I should think that's where he's camping – a grey-haired bloke with a goatee beard, alone in a blue-and-white Volks caravette. Would that be him?'

'Sounds like him.'

'Well, he looked harmless enough to me. Just another Continental across from Dieppe, taking advantage of the offseason fares.'

'Not the Traitor of Trouville.'

'Moossoo is pulling our legs, sir. And this bloke will have gone back by the weekend.'

'All the same, Caudry seems very disturbed. Enough to chase up here as though the devil were after him.'

'I'll talk to him, sir. He's getting worse.'

'Could there just possibly be something in it?'

'Not from where I'm sitting, sir. But I've had to hold his hand before.'

I said: 'Just to calm him down, can we keep a special eye on Caudry – say, an extra check on his premises, and now and then a car parked where he'll see it?'

Ringmer didn't sound thrilled.

'If you say so, sir. But I'd say a trick-cyclist was more what was needed.'

'Just till the weekend.'

'Right you are, sir. I should think we could run to that.'

I hung up and returned to the lounge. Caudry sprang to his feet as I entered. And for the second time, for the briefest of instants, the cat-like stare was back in his eyes. Then the flickering, the ingratiating smile.

'Monsieur has arranged it? I am to have protection?'

'Sit down, Caudry.'

'But it is arranged?'

I just knocked out my pipe. After a moment he sat again.

'I have been talking to Leyhurst, Caudry. There they seem to know you very well.'

'Oh monsieur, they do not understand, they are not men of the world like monsieur.'

'Let us say they have grave doubts about the authenticity of your story.'

He almost pouted.

16

'However,' I said. 'They are prepared to offer you a limited protection. Until this man Bernay returns to France. They will keep a special surveillance.'

'But, monsieur, this is not enough! That man is out there, waiting to strike.'

I shook my head.

'I can tell you quite certainly that Bernay did not follow you to London.'

'He . . . did not?'

'He did not. He was seen in Leyhurst a short while ago. He was leaving town to go to his camp-site. Like any other camper at this hour.'

His eyes were big.

'Monsieur, it is a trap! He wishes to lure me back to my shop. It is for the police that he puts on this act so that, later, I shall be unprotected.'

'You are letting your imagination run away with you.'

'Monsieur, I know the peril, and you do not.'

'The war is over, Caudry.'

'The war is never over. In the hearts of such men it is living still.'

I gestured.

'Have it which way you will. But all has been done that can be done. It is perfectly safe for you to leave, to drive back to Leyhurst, and to rest assured that an eye will be kept on you.'

'Then, monsieur, my blood will be upon your head.'

At which I lost patience.

'Just get out!'

'I go. You are a person of low intelligence.'

I seized his arm and ran him through the door.

But, back in the lounge, I couldn't help a quiet chuckle as I watched him turn his car, a beige Sierra estate. The whole interlude had verged on the comic from the moment he had pounded on my door. What had he really wanted? Attention? I couldn't honestly credit the Traitor of Trouville. Perhaps, after long sojourn in an alien land,

17

and now alone, he had begun to develop such delusions, when any fellow-countryman who looked at him sideways was liable to set him off. It was just that stare of his that troubled me, stopped the encounter from being truly comic. As though, behind all the absurdity, lurked something else: a glint of the sinister.

Anyway, not my affair; and the evening paper had just come through the door. He departed, the Frenchman, with a fresh squeal of tyres, and I sat down with the paper to await Gabrielle.

Over tea in the lounge, I told her about him.

'But he is Mr. Kirby in reverse,' said she.

'Mr. Kirby . . .?'

'But yes. Who keeps shop in Lisieux, and to whom I introduced you on a famous occasion.'

'The antique dealer?'

'Exactly. Who stays on in Normandy after the war. Who, also, is now a widower, and who has lost, you say, the art of making good tea.'

'Yes . . . Kirby.'

And I could see the parallel, relate the quirks of these two lonely men: two expatriates, each one stranded by life in the other's country. Kirby was liked in Lisieux. For an *Anglais*, a good fellow. But an *Anglais*: his French accented, his manners strange, behaviour eccentric. And was he, too, the prey of delusions, that sent him to harass the incredulous gendarmerie? And did Caudry, like Kirby, each Sunday morning, lay flowers and spend a vigil at his wife's grave?

'Only Kirby was P.B.I.,' I said. 'No connection with any underground.'

'P.B.I.?'

'Poor Bloody Infantry. Probably nothing in his past but a spell of jankers.'

'Oh, you talk nonsense!' Gabrielle said. 'And this matter of the Resistance is not funny. From my father I have heard the sad fate of the brave comrades of Trouville. These things happened, yes? Cannot be put away and forgotten. And, if friends of yours were taken out and shot, would not revenge stay in your heart for ever? You have not lived through such a business, my friend. This traitor has to fear the very birds in the air.'

'But we don't know that the tourist was the man. Just that he upset Monsieur Caudry.'

'Ah, why was I not here! I would have got the truth from this little shopkeeper.'

'Forty years can play tricks with the memory.'

'They remember each other. Is that not enough?'

'According to Caudry.'

'And upon each of their memories, will not the face of the other be engraven? The traitor, and he who can reveal him. They come face to face, and then? Those forty years are disappearing in a flash – oh yes, one can well believe it.'

'Meanwhile, the camper has gone back to his camp, and the police have set a watch on the shopkeeper.'

'And I am being too serious, you are going to say. While the toast I have made is growing cold.'

The television was indifferent that evening and we felt no inclination to sit up late. Before retiring I drew aside the curtains briefly, just to see the yellow leaves in the glow of the street-lamps. A wet world. A still world. Not a movement in the trees; not even a late-come car. It was Thursday, October 15th.

'Come to bed, you sad policeman!'

I think we were asleep by midnight. But an instant later, or so it seemed, we were awake again, with a thunder in our eyes like the roaring of a train.

'*Ecoutez*! What is that?'

'Put on the light.'

'There is no light!'

No; it was pitch black, within, without, though the heavy curtains were flogging like sails.

19

'The electric has gone!'

'There's a torch . . .'

Everything was getting in my way. I stumbled over I know not what, and at first I couldn't find the door to the hall. Then I had the torch. Now I could see them, the curtains that danced and tugged and flapped, and beyond the curtains, through the window, the bole of a lime tree, leaning preposterously.

'George, what is happening?'

'Wind . . . it's wind.'

'I think perhaps a nuclear bomb!'

'Wind . . .'

'It cannot be just wind!'

'Let me get this window shut . . .'

I dived in between the frantic curtains and succeeded in raising the sash. At the same moment the lime tree seemed to explode in white fragments. No more tree! And across the Walk I saw another go crashing down, then another, and another: like trampled grass the lime trees were falling. And the roaring went on, the train-like roaring, against which the crash of trees was as the crackling of paper.

'Oh, I think the house will come down!'

'Keep clear of the window. Stay by the wall.'

I went to grab the phone, but of course it was dead: I threw it down and returned to Gabrielle.

'Oh my love, I am afraid.'

'It will have to ease soon.'

'But if soon is too late?'

'We're safe as long as we stay inside.'

Were we? I had to believe so, as that roaring went on and on, as debris bounced and crashed outside, more trees shattered, the building shook. Just the wind? It was beyond experience, some terrible wrath chastising our world: the Valkyries riding by in the total blackness of the night. And two helpless animals, we clung together, tried to believe that we were safe.

20

The dawn came, and then we could see the total destruction lying without. Not a tree standing: rows of splintered stumps, and the parked cars buried beneath the layered trunks. Lime Walk had gone. There was too much sky. People crept from the houses to stare, stunned. At one stroke our familiar world had been dissolved and turned into rubbish that we couldn't believe.

'Oh, my dear . . . what has happened at Heatherings?'

No doubt we should hear in the course of the day. And it was then that I remembered the strange sadness I had been feeling the day before. Prescience? While, in my nostrils, was the sweet smell of the savaged trees.

2

Twenty dead was the first count given, heard on someone's portable radio. Twenty dead in the hurricane that had ripped across England from the Channel to East Anglia. The injured uncounted, the damage uncounted, towns large and small in a state of siege, an electricity blackout, telephones gone, no trains in and out of Liverpool Street Station. In London, Kew had taken a battering on a par with the slaughter in Lime Walk, but that was mere exotica, didn't tug at the heart-strings like our poor, outraged stumps. A century had gone into the making of that street: in our lifetimes we should not see it restored.

In fact the houses had come out of it well, those solid, complacent Victorian terraces, just a roof or two smashed by rogue trees, windows blown in, scarred brickwork, stonework. In our own case, a scatter of slates. The real damage lay under the rubbish. Forty or more cars, and none of them bangers, since in Lime Walk yuppies were the principal keyholders. Porsche and Audi and BMW, forty or more written off at a stroke. If there was any cheer in that morning it lay in my unscratched Rover, garaged in the mews.

'George . . . what do we do?'

A good question. We couldn't even make a pot of tea. Breakfast was muesli with the last of the milk after a cold, a very cold, wash-down. But as we chewed this, a whine of chainsaws was breaking out towards Church Street, and

22

shortly we could see a mobile crane stooping and weaving above the debris.

'This morning, shall you have to go in?'

Yes: the Yard didn't close down for hurricanes.

'Then what am I to do?'

'There isn't much you can do. Until they've cleared this mess away.'

'I shall search for a builder to mend our roof. And you, my friend, can perhaps ring Heatherings. For the rest I shall camp out in Bertie's hotel until the electrics come back on.'

It seemed a reasonable programme; we left that depressing scene together, a little inspirited by the spectacle of workmen loading a truck with debris at the bottom of the Walk. The tubes at least were running, and I got to my office barely an hour late. There I found a sad-faced Dutt drinking coffee with the Assistant Commissioner (Crime)'s secretary, Blondie.

'Did you cop it bad, sir?'

'Pretty bad. And you?'

'Every slate off the blinking roof. And all the builders round our way have got their phones off the hook.'

'Has the A.C. arrived?'

'No sir.'

'We've had a message from him,' Blondie said. 'He said to tell people that morning conference was scrubbed, and that he'd see them when and if he got here.'

The A.C. lives in Ashdown Forest among a lot of beech trees. At least, he used to.

'Has anything come in?'

'No sir.'

Presumably the villains were suffering too; or, more likely, with so many lines down, messages just weren't getting through. I took it upon myself to dismiss Dutt to attend to his chaos back in Tottenham, and then, being again in command of a working telephone, set about getting news out of Suffolk. First I tried our house, Heatherings, but that was a lost cause, and then the Reymerstons and the Capels, getting always the same open line. Finally I struck lucky with Wolmering police station, though the answering voice sounded distant and dream-like.

'Chief Superintendent Gently.'

'. . . sir?'

A moment later I was talking to Eyke. Things were bad, he told me: the town was still cut off, and he'd heard that the forest area was barely recognisable. No, there was no line to Welbourne and he could tell me nothing about my house. However they had hope of getting a road clear, and when that happened he would send out a patrol to check. So, small comfort; and straight after that I was hearing of calamities in Ashdown Forest.

'It's been hell, Gently – seventy grand's-worth of Bentley up the spout, not to mention the wife's Merc, and that's an E registration. This damned tree knocked the garage flat, and we've another one balanced on the roof . . . yes, the phone's back on, but short of a helicopter I'm stuck here.'

Well: even A.C.'s have their troubles.

'Anything fresh I should know about?'

'Nothing's in.'

'What's on your desk?'

'Just two reports to write.'

'I don't think you'll need to hang on, Gently, if nothing turns up after lunch. I daresay you've matters to see to yourself, so you've my permission to skive off. Understood?'

'Understood,' I said.

'But, good God, the damage here,' the A.C. said. 'The Seldon beeches went down, did you hear? They were one of the Seven Wonders of Sussex.'

It struck a note. 'Seldon?'

'The Seldon beeches, man. All flat. One fell on the campsite and killed a camper, a French tourist. Three-hundred-year-old trees, Gently, and now they've gone. Just like that.'

24

He hung up; I let him hang up. I wanted to think about what I'd heard. Till now, I hadn't given a second thought to my visitor of yesterday and his remarkable tale. A French camper killed at Seldon. Could it really be the same man? The alleged Resistance traitor, meeting his doom by Act of God? Bernay, if it were he, was last reported driving in the direction of the campsite, at the time, towards dusk, when campers are usually seeking their pitches; but it was only surmise that he had stayed there, or indeed was the only Frenchman on the site: as Ringmer had noted, the late-season tariffs brought an influx of Continentals. No, the odds were against: I smoked a pipe on it, got up and went to stare through the window. But in the end I came back to the desk, raised the phone and buzzed Ringmer.

'The French connection. Who was the camper who died last night at Seldon?'

'Oh, him.' Ringmer's tone suggested that dead Frenchmen were low priority. 'His name was Bernay all right, sir, just the way Moossoo was telling us. Pierre Maurice Bernay. We've just found his passport in the wreck.'

'What happened?'

'A tree fell on him, smashed his caravette flat. It took the firemen a couple of hours to cut his body out of the wreckage. Dead of course, sir. He was dressed, like he might have been intending to drive somewhere safer, but never got the chance. It all happened so quick, sir.'

'Has your doctor seen him?'

'He's rushed off his feet, just took a quick look and said he'd deal with him later. Sir, it's like a battlefield round here, and there's not much doubt about what killed the froggie.'

'Does Caudry know what's happened?'

'Yes sir. I had him in to identify the body. There was no ident on it, and it looked for a while that we mightn't recover any. There was a bit of a fire going on at the wreck, but luckily for us the other campers doused it. And now

25

we've got his passport and docs, and he's the bloke who Moossoo says he is.'

'What was Caudry's reaction?'

'Crossed himself, sir. Said something about the End of the Affair.'

'Was that all?'

'He was all on the shake. Like he was still scared of his own shadow. Do you reckon there was anything in that tale, sir?'

I shrugged to myself. 'Caudry believed it.'

'Bernay didn't come from Trouville, though. It says a place called Evreux on his passport.'

'Evreux?'

'What it says down here, sir.'

'Evreux is a town fifty miles from Trouville.' It also had a certain connection: which I was keeping to myself.

'Well, I don't know, sir,' Ringmer said. 'But either way it doesn't matter now. The bloke is dead, whatever he'd done, and that's got Moossoo out of my hair. Are things bad with you, sir?'

'Could be worse. What time will your doctor be examining the body?'

Ringmer paused, and I could imagine the wary expression coming over his face.

'You don't think there's been anything comic, sir?'

'Just for my satisfaction. I would like to know what the doctor makes of him.'

'It's pretty obvious, sir. The bloke was crushed flat. And you can't whistle up a wind like that.'

'Still. If you'll ring me back.'

Another pause!

'I'll grab Doctor Praed the next time he checks in, sir. But I can't say when that will be. We're still digging people out of the wreckage.'

I hung up, and tapped out my pipe. Then rang through for a mug of coffee.

So it wasn't my business, was it, and I banged away at a report: trying to be grateful that, at the Yard at least, I had heat, light and hot drinks. Much more to the point were affairs in Suffolk and the state of our beleaguered house, whose photograph, taken under smiling skies, sat at the corner of my desk. This evening, in the usual way, we would have set out for that peaceful home. I would arrive at the flat to find our bags in the hall and Gabrielle waiting with tea on the table. Then an hour's drive, a little more, and we would be pulling up at the door, where Mrs. Jarvis would have switched on the porch-light, and where a smell of cooking would emerge as she opened to us. Were they still waiting, those familiar Dutch gables? The twisty chimneys, the dormers, the pantiles? I thought of our copper beech and trembled: but at least it should have gone down clear of the house. Only now, now the prospect was bleak of our ever getting to Heatherings this weekend, with the roads blocked, the trains cancelled – yes, I had other things to think about!

I plodded on grimly with my work. The telephone stayed maddeningly silent. At lunch, the canteen was well-nigh deserted, just Pagram looking in for a word. But then, as I was returning to my office, I could hear the phone ringing inside. Eyke? Ringmer? I flung through the door and grabbed the instrument: at the other end, Gabrielle.

'My dear . . . did you hear the News at One?'

Like my own her thoughts had been with Heatherings. And the news was bad: it might be forty-eight hours before the main roads were cleared in parts of East Anglia. There, power cuts were the rule, while the telephones remained chaotic; all transport was disrupted, and British Rail could offer no hope.

'Have you news of our house?'

'Not yet.'

'Is it possible, my dear, that we shall get there?'

'Not very possible.'

'So I am thinking. So certain steps I have taken.'

27

'What steps?'

'If we remain here, shall we not need light and heat? And it is well that I think of this early, before the shop selling these things has been emptied.'

In effect she had raided the local hardware shop and commandeered their last portable gas-heater, along with two Camping Gaz lanterns, a box of candles and a picnic stove burning meta fuel. The gas-heater was a particular trophy; the shop's owner had been reserving it for himself.

'So now we are equipped, ha? No need to spend the night in Bertie's hotel. And this I tell you, I am ringing from the flat, where the telephone is back on.'

'And the roof?'

'A little man is up there. Him also I kidnapped at the store.'

But the News at One had carried another item to catch at her attention: among the reported storm casualties, mention of a French tourist, crushed by a falling tree, in Sussex.

'Could it not, by chance, be that Bernay who your Monsieur Caudry denounced as a traitor?'

It could; I told her what I knew; and at once she was pouncing on the critical point.

'Evreux? And he comes from Evreux? But so also does our good friend Frénaye! Is it not possible he knows of Bernay, and even if he is of a suspect character?'

'More than likely.'

'Then ring him, my friend, I am burning to know the truth of this matter. In France, too, they will wish to know that the traitor has been found, and now is dead.'

'I'm not sure we ought to meddle with this.'

'Monsieur George, you have meddled already. It is to you that this man is denounced, it is for you to discover, it may be, the truth. Have you not been conferring with the policeman at Leyhurst?'

28

'Simply establishing the facts.'

'The facts, ha – and is not the first of them whether or not Bernay was the traitor? I tell you, my friend, yes. To many people whose hearts still ache. This is an important duty you have, not least to your wife, whose father was a comrade. You will promise me, yes?'

'I'll talk to Frénaye. But he may never have heard of the man.'

'But you will promise?'

'Very well.'

'Then I hang up, my friend. And depart to shop for our meal.'

Would I have rung Frénaye in any case? It had been at the back of my mind. Though stationed now at Honfleur, that calm, polite policeman still had family in Evreux, whom he regularly visited. And Bernay was dead: it could do him no harm to pass on what I knew to Frénaye, who, moreover, if he found Caudry's allegations groundless, would be certain to keep them to himself. Still, I was hesitating, had a feeling that I would do well to let matters lie. Because Bernay might have relatives who would suffer? Perhaps. I wanted time to mull it over. So I went on with my report, and it was mid-afternoon before I reached for the phone again.

'Gendarmerie d'Honfleur?'

'Oui.'

'I wish to speak to Inspector Frénaye.'

'But – monsieur! – can it be you? We have been concerned – with this news of hurricanes – '

I could almost smell that tidy office, across the street from the coach station, with its outlook towards the Old Basin and the shuffle of tall houses. Bocasse, who had answered the ring, had probably a Gauloise in his mouth at that moment, while, upstairs in Frénaye's room, the aroma, would be that of pipe-tobacco.

'You have taken no harm, monsieur – yourself, and Madame Gabrielle? Here, it is remarkable, we have felt no wind at all.'

'No harm, Bocasse. May I speak to the Inspector?'

'But at once, monsieur. I put you through.'

And then, in Frénaye's soft tone: 'Monsieur, I cannot express my delight . . .'

I let him talk about the storm: apparently the local radio had been full of it, counting the millions of trees destroyed, estimating the damage in billions. And the dead, now twenty-one: the twenty-first being a Frenchman. At which point Frénaye paused, because the Inspector was nobody's fool.

'It is perhaps about this man you are ringing?'

'It is about this man, Frénaye.'

'Unfortunately, we do not yet have his name.'

'His name is Pierre Maurice Bernay.'

'Pierre Bernay!'

'Have you heard of him?'

'Monsieur George, this is terrible news. If it is Pierre Bernay of Evreux, I know both him and madame his wife. They are friends of my parents in Evreux. Alas, the poor lady. Has she been informed?'

'My colleagues should have taken care of that.'

'I am shocked, very shocked, Monsieur George. I cannot claim a close acquaintance, but I admired that man very much.'

'You admired him?'

'Who could not admire him? He was an artist of great talent. But, what counted for more in the eyes of Evreux, he was a great man of the Resistance.'

'The . . . Resistance?'

'But yes. He had a record second to none. Until the infamous D-Day betrayal, he was a leading member of the group at Trouville. At Evreux he is President of the Comrades, who will be grief-stricken to hear this news. Did you not know?'

30

'I have heard of a connection.'

'That man is a hero in Evreux.'

'I believe that he, alone, escaped the D-Day betrayal.'

'His luck, Monsieur George. It was proverbial.'

'Frénaye,' I said. 'I have met another man who claims to have escaped the D-Day betrayal. A man who since has lived his life in England. And who claims to have known Bernay.'

'Another man?'

'Another man. And he tells a strange story. A story I would not willingly believe, but which he insists is the truth.'

And then I gave it to him. At the other end, Frénaye listened without a word. But I could almost feel the indignation building up in that office in Honfleur. I told it straight. I told him of Caudry's terror at having recognised Bernay, of his certainty that Bernay would seek to kill him, as he had probably made away with others. It was blasphemy. I could feel it. And at last Frénaye burst out:

'What is this vile person's name?'

'Jean Caudry.'

'Monsieur George, let him not set foot in Evreux, that is all! Should the comrades hear such slander, he would be hung from the next lamp-post. And the gendarmes would not interfere. I, myself, would provide the rope.'

'Can you be so certain there is no truth in it?'

'The animal is lying in his throat.'

'It would be Bernay's word against his.'

'The word of a hero against that of a rat.'

'All the same, recognition does appear to have been mutual.'

'And who runs in terror to the police, Monsieur George? It is not Bernay, but this cowardly scoundrel who may, perhaps, have picked Bernay's pocket. Oh no. Oh no. I beg of you, keep this tale to yourself. Do not add it to the grief of the wife and to that of every Frenchman who knew Bernay. For myself it will be as though I had not

31

heard it, as though I do not know that such a wretch exists.'

'The name, Jean Caudry, rings no bells?'

'Till this moment my ears were not soiled by it.'

'He would appear to have been a resident of Trouville.'

'Then that town should go into mourning also.'

I left it at that. In his shock, his indignation, Frénaye probably didn't follow what I was driving at. Which may have been for the best, at least as far as Caudry was concerned. Two tales: conflicting tales. If one were true, what about the other? The weight appeared to be on Bernay's side . . . but both men had escaped from that trap in Trouville. Well: that could go on the back-burner: it was another aspect that bothered me. One pipe later the phone was back in my hand and I was ringing Leyhurst.

'Has the doctor made his examination yet?'

'Just a moment, sir. Doctor Praed is here now.'

A man with a curt, Scots accent, who wanted to be rid of me in short order.

'What are you asking?'

'Just the cause of death.'

'Death from multiple injuries. Do you wish me to describe them?'

'The immediate cause.'

'In my opinion, a semi-circular depressed fracture of the skull.'

'Have you examined the wreckage?'

'I have.'

'Did you find what might have caused the fracture?'

'I did not.'

'A blunt instrument-type injury?'

'You might call it that. But the diameter of the fracture exceeds that of a hammer.'

'Was there bleeding?'

'Minimum bleeding.'

'Would you care to comment on that?'

32

'I would have expected more blood. But I am not prepared to draw a conclusion.'

'In so many words, when he received the crush injuries, would the deceased have been alive or dead?'

'I repeat, I can draw no conclusion.'

'You rule out foul play?'

'My examination neither confirms nor excludes it.'

A bonny witness, that one. Ringmer came back on the line.

'So that's about it, sir. Nothing comic, just the poor devil buying one.'

'Have you questioned Caudry about his movements?'

'Well no, sir. We didn't have cause.'

'What about the other campers?'

'We had a word with them, sir, but all they remember is the crash. I did give Moossoo a talking to, and you won't be bothered by him again. Sorry again, sir, about that. But we all have our quota of nuts.'

And it wasn't my business was it, so who was I to press the matter further – on this day of all days, when police resources were stretched to breaking?

The phone again: it was Gabrielle.

'My dear, the telephone now works to Welbourne. And it is all right – Mrs. Jarvis has rung me! All we have lost is our big tree.'

'The copper beech?'

'And that is all. The house takes no damage. My dear, I am overwhelmed, I am thinking we shall never see our Heatherings again.'

'Did she mention the roads?'

'Aha, yes. I regret they are still blocked with fallen trees. But the house, the house is safe, except for a snow-board that falls down.'

'Power?'

'Alas, no power, but that they will deal with quickly, yes? And the fallen trees? Soon, it may be, we can be seeing our Heatherings again.'

Poor Gabrielle! Even more than for myself is that house the pivot our world turns on, where she flourishes: Mistress of Heatherings. But I didn't think we would see it that weekend.

'And you, my dear, you have kept your promise – you have rung our friend in Honfleur?'

'I kept my promise.'

'And?'

'It appears that Bernay is the toast of Evreux.'

'Ha? The toast?'

'There he is regarded as a great hero of the Resistance, and Frénaye was ready to knock me down for suggesting anything different.'

'Then – he is not a traitor?'

'Apparently not. In Evreux he was President of the comrades. He leaves a widow and, according to Frénaye, his death will plunge the town in mourning.'

Gabrielle was silent a moment.

'My friend, this gives me to think. Unless your Monsieur Caudry is weak in the head, we have a strange mystery here.'

'After all, that may be the solution.'

'It is very interesting,' Gabrielle said.

I finished my reports, nothing had come in, and so, to use the A.C.'s term, I skived off. I returned to a Lime Walk still skirling with chain-saws and the lamentations of yuppies over a score of bent cars. But progress had been made. As far as the flat the Walk had been cleared of fallen trees, leaving ankle-deep litter in places and the bent cars afore-mentioned. Tarpaulins clung to damaged roofs, glaziers were dealing with gaping windows, while sundry men on ladders were replacing shed slates. And overall, still this stunned air, still the witness of the shattered stumps; of a violence unbelievable. And the smell of slaughtered trees.

Gabrielle opened the door to me in triumph – *voilà*! A pot of fresh-made tea. The meta fuel stove worked, and

34

the gas-heater could be used to heat up soup. We would survive, yes? But the rooms had changed, seemed more naked: outside the windows, a gap of sky where once a hundred-year-old tree had stood. And then, as the light faded, as the chain-saws one by one packed in, the lounge becoming a strange, shadowed place, which the Gaz lanterns seemed unwilling to illuminate. The dark ages come again – no radio, no TV; while Bruisyard '86, at room temperature, cheered but thinly the cold meats that followed the soup.

'My dear,' Gabrielle said at last. 'We shall not go to Heatherings, am I right?'

'In the morning the news may be better.'

'But, you think we do not go.'

'It seems unlikely.'

'Also, the power will come back here we know not when, we have no cooking, and the gas-heater, though successful, also smells.'

'You think we should go to Bertie's hotel?'

'Alas, we are too late. By lunchtime the Upwardly people had taken it over, along with some other accommodation I telephoned.'

'Then?'

Her firm eyes fixed mine. 'I wish conversation with that shopkeeper in Leyhurst. He shall tell me that tale to my face, aha, so that I shall judge if he is a liar.'

I thought about it, shrugged. 'He gave me the impression of being God's own liar.'

'But you are *Anglais*, my friend, and he is French, and moreover, you say, in a state of terror. Thus you could receive a wrong impression. But I, I am French, and a Norman too. Perhaps it is I know the type of this man. Perhaps also I am brought up in the legend of the comrades, have a certain instinct, an alertness.'

'And suppose you do nail him down as a liar?'

'Do not pretend to be a fool, my friend! Two men escape that slaughter at Trouville, one is fêted as a hero,

35

one crosses La Manche. It could be that the hero is a traitor and the exile the one person who knows it. And that is the most likely? Oh no, oh no! And this I do not need to tell a clever policeman.'

And her eyes were sharp in the pervading gloom, which seemed to extend to the very mantles of the lanterns.

'It could be just that Caudry suffers from delusions.'

'Yet he recognises this man correctly. After forty years. And how? Unless it is the face of all others that he fears.'

'He had perhaps injured this man in some way.'

'In what way?'

'Who knows? Perhaps seduced his wife.'

'You are clutching at straws, I think. For that, would he have told a tale of Resistance betrayal? And see, he knows so much, about Bernay, about that night in Trouville. They are not delusions, these things, and of them he shows a dangerous knowledge.'

'It could still have been the way he says.'

'And that is what we shall discover. We shall go to this shop where is sold tents and gas and there judge which is the truth.'

'This, too, could be dangerous knowledge.'

'Oho. When the police know also? I must have the truth, my friend. I, the daughter of a comrade.'

'In any case the roads are probably blocked.'

'Not so. I have telephoned the RAC.'

'And the hotels, full.'

'A provisional booking we have at a hotel in Leyhurst High Street.'

Had we indeed! I chewed it over. I doubted whether we would learn very much from Caudry. But a chat with Ringmer might not come amiss, under the guise of filling him in about Bernay. Because I hadn't liked that doctor's report: it sounded too much like some others I had dealt with.

'This booking then – I shall confirm it?'

'Don't expect too much, Gabrielle.'

'A talk face to face, that is all. After that, we will behave like tourists.'

We went to bed early because there was precious little else to do. In the gloom surrounding those lanterns, our books had become suddenly unappealing.

3

The power hadn't come back on by the morning, but the picnic stove provided tea and hot water. A pale sun lit the devastation without, the first we had seen since the storm. The chain-saws were moaning at first light. I put through an early call to Mrs. Jarvis: the power wasn't back there either, but there were hopes of a road being cleared before night. Hot tea, cold breakfast, and we were on the road before nine, with the Rover's heater a luxury that we'd barely noticed at other times.

And the havoc began to appear as we left the town behind – trees, walls, entire buildings collapsed, as though the country had been under a bombardment. At one point the road threaded an area of forest, and there the damage was absolute. Whole sections of pines, acre upon acre, lay flattened under mounds of impenetrable debris. Sawn butts projecting towards the road showed where the clearers had done their job, and sawdust was strewn along the verges. While the smell of slaughter pervaded the car.

'It is sad. So sad.'

Even the soft sun couldn't put a gloss on it. Silent, inanimate trees were suddenly presented as stricken creatures.

'And under such trees, poor Bernay . . .?'

'Under a beech tree. Very large.'

'He could have known nothing, perhaps?'

'Nothing. It was instantaneous.'

Gabrielle was silent for a space. Then:

'My dear, this point you do not touch on. But is it certain, quite certain, that it was in this way Bernay lost his life?'

'The local police are of that opinion.'

'But you?'

I drove some more.

'There may be a question.'

'Aha. Of something that happens before the crash?'

I nodded.

'And in connection with the shopkeeper?'

'At the moment, there is no evidence of that.'

'But a question, yes?'

'A small question.'

She let at least another half-mile go by before saying, in a low voice:

'Then, I would not be that man.'

I said: 'Just remember that we have no evidence.'

But Gabrielle was silent again.

So we drove on through that ravaged landscape, Surrey giving way to Sussex, and the green line of the Downs beginning to shape before us. A matter of sixty miles, no more. We were running into Leyhurst before eleven. I drove directly to the Swinburne Hotel, where, after booking in, we ordered coffee and hot scones, and settled with them in the lounge.

'My friend, this is better than the smell of gas-heaters!'

From the lounge, we were looking down Leyhurst High: a pleasant, sloping street with a medley of Georgian and Victorian shopfronts. Leyhurst is modest but long in history, has a castle-keep, the remains of a priory; is set in a lap of the Downs with the Channel not far. From the earliest times, a favourite resort. And seemingly undamaged by the late catastrophe.

'It is in this street . . .?'

In fact we were staring at it, but a few yards down, on the side opposite: a double-fronted shop with window displays that included an erected ridge-tent: The Camping Shop.

39

As we watched, two customers emerged, one humping a brown-paper parcel.

'And, in there . . .'

She was tense, my Gabrielle, dressed today in a severe black two-piece.

'We will finish our coffee, then confront this man?'

I shook my head. 'Not quite yet.'

'Not yet?'

'First, I must introduce myself to the locals. But even before that I intend to make a visit to the scene of the tragedy.'

'Ha – you shall find something there?'

'Probably not. But it's worth a try.'

'And then, with this, you confront the shopkeeper?'

'It may assist in my inquiries.'

'You are too professional, my friend. Myself, I should walk straight through that doorway. I would stare this man in the eye and defy him to tell me his falsehoods.'

'He would nevertheless tell them.'

'Then I give them the lie. I would thrust them back down his throat.'

'But then you would be no wiser than before.'

'You tell me? But I, I would know which was the traitor.'

'Drink up your coffee.'

'Aha. You are not the daughter of Jacques Orbec.'

It was almost light-hearted, but not quite. The cup was quivering in Gabrielle's hand. Uneasily I had watched her involvement in this affair growing increasingly more intense. She was right, she was French, I was English, didn't have the root of the matter in my blood, was seeing it largely from a professional standpoint. But suppose – for Trouville – one read Eastbourne, or Brighton?

We finished our coffee and went through to the car, which was parked in the yard, out of sight of that shop.

Nor did we have to pass the shop on the short run out to Seldon, a drive extended by a detour around a section of road still blocked. Seldon was on a slope of the Downs, with the park and monster beeches at its elbow; that is, they had been. Now, our first hint of them was a barrier of cones and the detour sign. Of those giants, not one was left standing. We came at last to the place where they lay. Once more, a battlefield, but here made the more poignant by the size, the beauty of the slain. Beeches are feminine. Smooth-skinned, soft-limbed. Like fallen goddesses they lay there. Beset by pygmies with wailing chain-saws, cutting them down to mortal size. For a space one could but stand and stare and feel a sadness near to tears.

'Look, my dear . . .'

At the extreme edge of the piled trees, a notice cast to one side: Camping Club/Seldon/This is a Limited Facility Site. Well, it was even more limited now. The sign marked a lane, cut up by heavy vehicles, bordered by a stout beech hedge and leading into a sort of laager of about half an acre. At the far end a tent was still pitched, with an estate-car lined up beside it; at the near end, the ravaged remains of one of the beeches and houghed-up ground, stained with oil. It had been the last beech in the grove, falling perversely, exactly there.

'Oh, poor Monsieur Bernay!'

Clearly, he would never have stood a chance. The sawn-up sections of the mighty trunk measured five feet or more in diameter. It would have crushed a tank, much less a caravette, and a crater showed where the vehicle had stood. Near it lay a dented Volkswagen hub-plate, and shattered glass was trampled in the oily mud.

'Then . . . he died in the storm.'

'That's the theory.'

'But my dear, what doubt can there be? His caravan is flattened like an old can – only see where it is forced into the ground.'

'It may have been so.'

'Alas. For his death, at least, we cannot blame the shopkeeper.'

I poked around in the vicinity of the crater, not knowing what I looked for; and finding nothing. Any clues there might have been had departed with the wreck, been trampled out, or vanished under the rubbish. If indeed there had been comic business then Caudry had been lucky beyond his dreams.

The camper emerged from his tent and came over, a small, grey-faced man, clad in jeans. For a moment he too stood gazing at the crater, then:

'Friends of that poor sod, are you?'

'I'm a policeman.'

'Ah. Didn't know, the lady along with you and all. Had he got any people?'

'A wife. Were you camped here for the night before last?'

'All the week.'

'Can you remember what happened?'

'It was me who put out the fire.'

He pointed to an extinguisher that lay on its side by a stand-pipe. Over at the tent a blonde-haired woman, also in jeans, stood watching us.

'Did you have any conversation with the man?'

'Well you couldn't exactly call it that, him not speaking much English and me without a word of frog. But yes, we tried a few words. You do when you're on the same site. Told me where he came from, but I can't remember the name.'

'Did he have any visitors?'

'Not except the warden, when he came to collect the fee.'

'Did anyone enquire after him – perhaps another Frenchman?'

The camper shook his head.

On the Friday night, he said, Bernay returned to the site soon after four o'clock, parked his van at the usual spot and set about getting a meal. There were only three of them on the site, Bernay, himself, and a couple with a camp-van. Later that evening he'd met Bernay at the tap, where they'd both gone to fill their containers; it was raining, and Bernay had made some joke about English weather.

'Never knew it was the last time I'd speak to him. There wasn't a breath of wind, just then.'

Rain makes campers anti-social and he and his wife had retired early, though they could faintly hear the Frenchman's radio going until, at a guess, ten-thirty. And then they slept. And then they woke: with the great roaring in their ears, with the tent canvas flogging, the sound of successive thunderous crashings.

'It was like the end of the bloody world. I was in the blitz, but it was never like that.'

In moments the tent was blown flat and they were struggling in a black nightmare, to emerge at last, clad only in night-clothes, at first crouching for shelter behind the car.

'I'd got our handlamp. I saw the camp-van go. I think the woman hurt her arm. The froggie's lifting roof was down and I thought he'd bailed out.'

'You didn't see him.'

'No. Nor there wasn't a light in the van. I swung the lamp about, looking for him. He couldn't have been asleep, not through that lot.'

'The van's roof had collapsed.'

'I'm telling you. Perhaps it hit him and knocked him cold.'

And then the climax of that terror, a slow, crashing, grinding thunder, with the ground seeming to leap under them and the air thick with flying debris. What had happened? The dancing beam of the handlamp was showing a scene that had changed utterly, in a moment had become somewhere else, a chaos of nowhere and violence.

'The wife was screaming but you couldn't hear it. The other couple were diving under their car. And all you could see up here was a bloody great mound of rubbish. The van was under it, I knew, and I was praying to God

43

the frog had cleared out, and then I saw some flames coming from it and I scrambled up and belted over here.'

He'd grabbed up the regulation extinguisher with which all campsites are equipped, struggled over boughs and debris and played the jet on the flames. Fool or hero? Around him the trees were still coming down, debris flying past his head. But he got the flames under control.

'You could see the van then?'

'Oh Christ yes. Like it was bent up round the tree. And the poor sod in it, with the tree across him. It must have crushed him into pulp.'

'Unlike you, he was dressed.'

'That's what I couldn't make out.'

'He was lying on the floor?'

'What was left of it. His head and shoulders was all I could see.'

'Face down?'

'Yes. If I'd seen his face I'd have thrown up.'

Dead, and nailed down under a tree that an army couldn't have lifted off him: the camper had thrown down the extinguisher and run back to crouch with his wife. But as the nightmare wore on, as the crashing of trees grew less frequent, the urge to take some action had become irresistible. Finally, he'd left his wife with the other couple and found his way to the village, though even there, sans phone, sans power, they'd had to wait for a police patrol to reach them.

'And you stayed on here – after that?'

'Wanted to see it through, didn't we?'

The camp-van couple had left the next day, the lady with her arm in a sling.

'I would like you to think back to that evening when you last spoke to the Frenchman. Did he seem quite normal – not upset about anything?'

The camper stared.

'Normal I'd say. Except I was keeping him waiting in the rain. What wasn't normal was him being dressed and still in his van when the tree hit it.'

'Could he have dressed, intending to drive the van clear?'

'But Christ, there wasn't any time for that. It hit us all of a sudden, didn't it. He should have been out of that van like a jack-rabbit.'

'So then he never went to bed.'

'I can only tell you what we know. His radio was going till around ten-thirty, some froggie station. I heard the announcer.'

'At that time, a still night.'

'Just the rain coming down.'

'Could you hear the couple in the camp-van?'

'No. They turned in before us.'

'Perhaps vehicles on the road.'

'Well there you are. You don't take any notice of them.'

'A vehicle that stopped?'

He stared again.

'Just what are we getting at, squire?'

I said: 'I want you to remember if a vehicle stopped here at some time on Thursday evening. Probably rather late. After you and your wife had gone to bed.'

'And if it did?'

'Did one?'

Slowly he began to nod. 'The wife heard it, not me. I was off in the land of dreams.' He turned and called to his wife: 'Mave!' The blonde-haired lady reluctantly joined us. 'Mave, this gentleman is a copper, and wants to know about that car you thought you heard.'

A car: she'd heard it in the lane, on the other side of the beech hedge, heard it turn in from the road and park, heard a door closed softly, not slammed. Had thought it was some benighted camper arriving, but none had appeared on the site.

'Could you estimate the time?'

45

'Don't know about that. It was after we'd turned in. Fred had dropped off, but I was still reading my book. After ten, say. Quarter-past. I put the light out at ten-thirty.'

'Could you hear the Frenchman's radio playing?'

'Oh yes, I could still hear that. It was when he switched it off I looked at my watch, and put the light out.'

'At ten-thirty.'

'Yes.'

'Did you stay awake after that?'

'A bit.'

'What else did you hear?'

'Well, nothing. Except maybe the froggie closing his door.'

'You heard that?'

'It's a slider, isn't it. You can always hear them. Closed it nice and quiet, he did, but I could hear it all the same. Daresay he'd gone outside, you know, before he turned in.'

'And the car. Did you hear it leave?'

She shook her head. 'I was just dropping off. May have heard it, I don't know. The next thing all hell was breaking loose.'

'Between the time it parked, and the time the van's door closed: do you remember hearing anything then?'

She thought, but shook her head again. 'I was reading my book, wasn't I?'

They had already been told off for the inquest: Fred and Mavis Streeter, from Stepney. If they had no suspicions before, I'm afraid I was leaving them with some now. We left them standing thoughtfully together, by the crater, the debris. As we turned into the lane I saw Fred stoop to pick up the hub-cap.

'My dear,' Gabrielle murmured. 'That was professional indeed. At first I am convinced that Bernay died by accident, but now I do not know what to think.'

'We still have no link-up with Caudry.'

46

'But with a person who is unknown, ha? I think if that woman had looked out of her tent she would have had other reasons to scream.'

Only we didn't know that either; the fabric of circumstance might well have been innocent – the car, say, that of a courting couple, the closing van door a domestic event. All that was standing out proud was the discovery of the body fully-dressed, and Bernay's inexplicable insensibility to the havoc proceeding without. For that, no innocent explanation was available. Or none that came readily to hand.

We drove back sombrely, each with our thoughts, and parked in a slot outside the police station.

'I didn't expect to see you out here, sir. Moossoo hasn't been pestering you again, has he? I had a talk with him yesterday, and I thought I'd straightened him out.'

Six foot, solid build, porridgey features and thrusting grey eyes. Hair worn in a style. And Ringmer was a bit of a trendy dresser.

'By chance, I know someone who knew Bernay and could give me information about him. I thought it was worth passing on, and perhaps another chat with Monsieur Caudry. My wife, who is French and comes from those parts, wishes to speak with him also.'

Watchful eyes that were growing more watchful.

'Are you saying Bernay was who Moossoo says he was, sir?'

'Apparently quite the reverse. In Evreux, Bernay is regarded as a Resistance hero. His exploits were famous, and he alone escaped the Trouville executions.'

'But Moossoo recognised him, sir.'

'Just so. And he recognised Caudry.'

'And then Moossoo starts bawling for us to protect him.'

'To the extent of seeking me out in town.'

Ringmer's eyes slid aside for a moment.

'I don't know, sir. It's a queer business. Someone's got to be right about this, but the way I see it, it doesn't matter now.'

'Monsieur,' Gabrielle said hotly. 'It matters very much to some people. To people whose sons, husbands, fathers were shot in cold blood in that courtyard at Trouville. There is a traitor and we wish to know him. This must not be swept beneath carpets.'

'I can understand your feelings, ma'am – '

'They are the feelings of many people.'

'But it did happen a long time ago.'

'In France, monsieur, it happened yesterday.'

'And anyway, the man is dead.'

'Ha. The man. But who is the man?'

Ringmer was beginning to look uncomfortable.

'We have just come from Seldon,' I said. 'Two of the campers are still there. I had a word with them about what happened.'

'You did, sir?'

I had of course not the smallest of briefs to do so. A name from the Yard or not, I was playing games in Ringmer's manor, and in the politest way possible he could have told me to sling my hook. It must have passed through his mind, but he resisted the temptation. Because, after all, a nutter from his patch had come bugging me.

'Fred and Mavis Streeter. You'll have talked to them already.'

'The Streeters, yes sir. They saw the tree fall. It was Streeter who reported the incident.'

'I went over a few points with them. Mrs Streeter heard a car park in the lane. That was around ten-fifteen, when the Streeters were already in bed.'

'A car?'

'Someone closed the door quietly. Bernay had the radio playing in his van. At ten-thirty the radio was switched off and the van door was closed, also quietly.'

Ringmer was staring as though he'd been slapped.

48

'That car could have been courters, sir. The lane is a favourite spot for them, we've had complaints from the warden.'

'That is of course possible. But then we come to the storm breaking. It collapsed the Streeters' tent and they had to struggle out and seek refuge behind their car. Another couple were in the same plight. No one could have slept through the commotion. Yet there was no sign of life from Bernay, though his lifting roof had been flattened.'

'The roof could have knocked him out, sir.'

'Again possible. But we find the body fully dressed.'

'So he was getting ready to drive out of there.'

'Only no one else had time to dress.'

'Then perhaps he never went to bed, sir. Froggies – begging your pardon, ma'am – mayn't do things like us. Or like he just lay down and dropped off, that's happened to me before today.'

'And the storm never woke him?'

'Perhaps it did, sir, but he was knocked cold when the roof blew down.'

'Have you Praed's report handy?'

I faced a moment of denial in the wary eyes; then he fumbled through papers in a tray and pushed a report sheet across. And there it was, among horrific crush-injuries to the middle torso and legs: a semi-circular depressed fracture of the right parietal, circa 7cm in diameter. Immediate cause of death: the fracture. E.T.D. between midnight and 2am; but there Praed was probably covering himself after his chat on the phone with me. I took a pen, underlined the fracture, passed the sheet back to Ringmer.

'Any item of the roof structure that could have caused that?'

'The roof was shattered by the tree, sir.'

'But it would be the usual sort of glass-fibre roof with side-curtains, supported by light metal struts?'

'That sort of thing, sir.'

'So what caused the fracture?'

'Well – anything, sir. In a job like that. I was at the scene before they started in, and no sort of injury would have surprised me.'

'But a specific, semi-circular fracture. Seven centimetres is about three inches. Requiring a solid, cylindrical object. Striking the skull at a slight angle.'

'It might have been a bough.'

'Not possible.'

'He could have struck his head when he went down, sir.'

'Then on what? Dr. Praed inspected the wreck and was unable to make a suggestion. What we are looking at here is a classic blunt-instrument injury, one that might have been caused by a hammer if the diameter didn't rule it out. But, a blunt instrument.'

Ringmer was looking sick.

'So you're saying we should treat this as murder, sir?'

'At the moment I'm saying you should bear it in mind. And perhaps make a few additional inquiries.'

'You think that car belonged to chummie.'

I nodded. 'It fits the rest. At ten-fifteen he parks in the lane and makes his way to the site. It's raining and black as pitch, just glows of light from the Streeters' tent and the van. Now either chummie lures Bernay outside or hangs about waiting his chance, but the moment Bernay sticks his head out chummie clobbers him with the blunt instrument. He shoves the body back in the van, switches off lights, radio, eases the door shut, and then he's away. And the storm comes to cover up his handiwork.'

Ringmer's stare was doubtful.

'Still circumstantial, sir.'

'But the injury isn't.'

'I don't know, sir. Dr. Praed gives the E.T.D. as between midnight and 2am.'

'I think you'll find that figure negotiable.'

50

'Perhaps I'll be taking another look at the wreck. With all due respect, sir, we've got enough on our plate not to go about looking for trouble.'

I shrugged. 'That has to be your decision.'

'Oh, you English policemen!' Gabrielle burst out. 'Can you not understand that you are dealing with the Resistance, and that your silly little rules go all by the board? Bernay is a traitor, says this shopkeeper, and goes about in fear of his life. And if it is true, do you think it stops there? Oh no, my friends. Oh no.'

Ringmer's English expression was very English.

'We can't just take things for granted, ma'am.'

'Aha, for granted. Then let me tell you something. Is it not on Wednesday that first the shopkeeper sees Bernay?'

'It was Wednesday, ma'am.'

'So. He sees this traitor, this traitor sees him. And only to the English police does he tell this thing, who know nothing, and will not believe him? Miss Fanny Adams! Before even this he is telephoning the comrades in France, and it is known that this man, until now thought a hero, is he who betrayed his group in Trouville. And the comrades will sit on their hands, ha? They will say what a naughty boy? Monsieur, who betrays the Resistance has not long to say his prayers.'

Ringmer was staring helplessly from Gabrielle to me.

'You're saying it was the frogs – beg pardon, ma'am! – the frenchies who came over and knocked him off?'

'Monsieur, they would not merely cross La Manche, such a man they would pursue to the world's end. But, it may not be true, yes, that Bernay is a traitor at all, and, *au contraire*, the traitor is he who calls wolf. And is that better reason to shut one's eyes? Oh, that shopkeeper does well to be fearful! Either Bernay will seek justice himself, before catching his ferry, or carry advice to those who will. Already, perhaps, too late, and the word has gone out on the shopkeeper, but, whichever, he dare not wait, Bernay must die, and die he does.'

'Well, it could be as you say, ma'am – '

'Was not the shopkeeper in fear of his life?'

'All the same, we've known Moossoo a long time – '

'And is Bernay not dead, with foulest play suspect?'

'We'll look into it, ma'am, I promise! I'll go through that wreck with a fine-tooth comb. But we need a little bit more than we've got before we start throwing charges about.'

'Me, you do not believe either, ha?'

'Just that we have to do it our way, ma'am. But we'll do it. If there's been any comic business, we won't let anyone get away with it.'

'Ha,' Gabrielle said.

I said: 'In the meantime, you'll have no objection to us talking to Caudry?'

'Oh no, sir. Only too glad. As you know, I'm pushed to the limit for manpower.'

'I will, of course, report back.'

'I'm sure we can rely on you, sir.'

'And you, perhaps, will take a statement from the Streeters, who intend to strike camp this afternoon.'

Ringmer swallowed.

'I'll see to it, sir. If I have to go out there myself.'

On which tidy note we left.

'My dear,' Gabrielle said. 'I'm not pulling legs about the comrades. I know these people. It is a matter of honour with them. Too easily it could be as I have said. And if it was they who served justice on Bernay, by now they will be back in France, in Evreux.'

At noon the sun was quite warm on this second day after the storm, and the breeze gentle, from the sou'west. We drove the short distance back to the hotel yard. And set out across the High to interview a shopkeeper.

4

Like any other strollers we gazed in the windows of The Camping Shop in Leyhurst High. Now we could see that the small tent formed part of an end-of-season sale. The major display in the window was of waxed jackets, along with derriboots, shooting-sticks, game-bags; that in the other window was of skis and ski-kit, with a corner for sweaters and a coat in sheepskin. Gabrielle stared with appraising eyes.

'This compatriot does good business. He carries a good stock, his prices are keen. I do not think he will want for a few francs.'

Indeed, a Jaguar of current date-letter was parked on the double yellow lines outside, and we could see Caudry hovering about a couple who were trying on the sheepskin coats.

We entered to the clang of a doorbell; at once the staring eyes whipped towards us. But the tradesman in Caudry triumphed, and he went on attending to his customers.

'The fit is too close for madame . . . madame would like to try the next size upwards? Regard the flawless skin, monsieur . . . this is the quality that others envy . . .'

Gabrielle sniffed. 'The fellow is a gigolo. In my own business, I would not employ him.'

'Nonetheless, I think he will sell those coats.'

'In selling at a counter, dignity is all.'

We wandered around the establishment, dogged by the smell of the sheepskin coats. Clearly camping was

over for that year, and a small display of gear was all
marked-down – stoves, pegs, nylon cord, a couple of
sleeping-bags on a rack; and something else that took my
interest: but I let it lie for the moment. Caudry had judged
well, was left with little, had now stocked-up for winter and
Christmas. I, too, liked the look of the sheepskin coats, the
Norwegian sweaters, the gloves.

'A fur hat, madame – ah, *parfait*! . . . Access, Visa
. . . I take all, monsieur.'

And every moment an eye on us, a stare that went so
ill with his patter. But he made the sale. Half-a-grand's
worth of sheepskin departed the shop in two parcels, and
he saw his punters to the Jaguar, towards which, ever
more slowly, a traffic-warden was mooching. Complais-
ant Leyhurst! The Jaguar slid away, Caudry hesitated, as
though in thought. Then he turned back abruptly into the
shop, the stare hard, the withered features determined.

'Monsieur, I regret that I close for lunch. I must ask
monsieur to return this afternoon.'

'Put the bolt on the door, Caudry.'

'I cannot serve you now.'

I slid the bolt on the door myself, and turned the card
from Open to Closed.

And, as though at the touch of a button, Caudry was the
fawning shopkeeper again: tittering as though I had played
a joke, and writhing his long, lean body.

'Monsieur, but this is so unexpected! I do not think I
shall be honoured by a visit from monsieur . . .'

'We have some talking to do, Caudry.'

'But of course. Monsieur will have heard of the tragic
happening . . .'

'The death of Bernay.'

'Ah, that terrible storm!'

'The fear of whom sent you to me in London.'

'Monsieur, how can I express my regret at such a foolish
action on my part?'

'Just – foolish?'

'But yes. I am an idiot. I am overwrought by what I think I remember. But as monsieur said, it is forty years since, in such a time the brain is perhaps playing tricks. Monsieur understands this, perhaps comes to forgive me for my rude behaviour in his house.'

I shook my head.

'No, Caudry.'

'Monsieur, my regret is great, is profound.'

'It won't do.'

'I bite back all my words, and, if there is some small way . . .'

I went on shaking my head.

'Monsieur, I beg that you forget my folly.'

'I have a friend in France, Caudry.'

'A friend . . .?'

'A friend who knew Bernay. A friend in La Normande. A friend from Evreux.'

The stare couldn't have been more ghastly, the lined cheeks more suddenly pale.

'Monsieur . . . what is it you are saying?'

'I am saying that you lied about Bernay.'

'It may be . . . my memory . . .'

'You lied. You identified Bernay as a traitor.'

He wrung his hands.

'I do not know. In all these years, who can remember? Monsieur, I tell these stories to amuse my customers . . . I am famous . . . but, as to the truth . . .'

I said: 'Yes? As to the truth?'

'Monsieur, I am an ageing man. I have, perhaps, more invention than memory, I tell tales that people wish to hear.'

'You came to tell me a tale?'

'Say I was drunk! One thousand times I am regretting . . .'

'You weren't drunk, Caudry, and you told me a lie. That is what my friend from Evreux is saying.'

'Bernay is dead, monsieur.'

'Very dead.'

'Then let his bones rest!'

'No.'

He made a little whining noise and ducked his head away. I glanced at Gabrielle. She was watching Caudry with an intent, scowling gaze. Just then a customer rattled the door-handle: Caudry jerked violently, made signs for the man to go. The fellow went, muttering. Caudry turned again to me.

'Then it is not a lie – no! Why must I pretend about this man? It is all the truth that I told you, let it stay with him in his grave.'

'Bernay was the traitor.'

'Yes.'

'Though his friends, his comrades, call him a hero?'

'They are abused, monsieur, he has fooled them, just as he fooled the comrades at Trouville. Was not his trade deception? Would he have survived, if not an adept? A rope and a placard round his neck would have been the reward of a false step. And I, monsieur, I, the only man who could denounce him, gone, vanished in the invasion. Why shall he not tell the great lie?'

I said: 'And, in forty years, you have never been back to Trouville?'

'To that place of such memories? Never! Monsieur must think I am made of stone.'

Gabrielle said: 'Though a traitor still lived?'

'Oh, madame, can I know that? It may be long since that the comrades have punished him, or perchance *les Chleuhs*, because he knew their secrets.'

Gabrielle stepped closer. 'Monsieur, look at me! I am a native of Rouen. Trouville I know. Evreux. And my father was Jacques Orbec.'

'You are Orbec's daughter . . .?'

'*Oui*. And of these matters I know many things. I am not to be fooled by a teller of tales or by the slander of a

56

brave comrade. Bernay is dead and cannot talk, but you, monsieur, both can and will. You shall tell what happened at that time in Trouville, and, monsieur, you shall tell the truth.'

'Madame, you are too young to know –'

'Remember who was my father, monsieur.'

'He was not there, in Trouville –'

'In the Place Barthel, he hears all.'

And Caudry was shrinking from those steady eyes, his thin lips gaping, his breathing quickened. Another would-be customer peered through the door, but this time Caudry didn't see him.

'Madame, I am a man alone. Bernay, it appears, has many friends. Already, I open my mouth too far. And across *La Manche* is but a step.'

'But, monsieur, you did open your mouth. And now the truth you shall tell.'

'It may endanger me, madame.'

'The truth, monsieur. Or admit that you lie.'

'So, if I lied –'

'Then,' Gabrielle said, 'who is the traitor, monsieur shopkeeper?'

One more customer rattled the door: making Caudry jump as though he'd been shot.

His long, lean body was shaking and he looked as though he wanted to sit down. But other than a picnic-chair in a display the shop had no seat to offer. He felt for the counter, leaned against it, stared a while at the rack of sheepskins. A man afraid. His fear locked in him. Yet somehow, one could feel small pity.

'I was very young . . . eighteen, madame. At that age one does foolish things. I am an errand-boy for a grocer and so have a bicycle at my service.'

'Aha. And which grocer is that?'

I was watching his eyes: fear was very real in them.

'In the Rue d'Orleans . . . I cannot recall . . . but

yes, the owner's name was Papin. This shop you know, madame?'

'Such a shop is found in the Rue d'Orleans.'

'Doubtless all is changed, there is another owner, but, at that time, a Monsieur Papin. To this man I am apprenticed, and, in my vocation, visit many houses. In one such lives Pierre Bernay, who is a clerk in the office of the Mayor. It is the Occupation, madame, Bernay is a comrade, and, it is not long, he finds a use for me. The telephone is unsafe, *les Chleuhs* have commandeered the cars, but who notices an errand-boy in a striped apron? So, I too am sworn-in a comrade, and beneath my groceries go other matters – guns, ammunition, explosives, beside coded messages in my receipt-book. If I am caught, I am tortured and shot. But I am eighteen and easily led.'

'At eighteen, you are sworn-in a comrade?'

'But yes, madame. Perhaps your father –'

'You are introduced to their place of meeting, and can name others beside Monsieur Bernay?'

His hands were gripping the counter.

'It is long ago, the names of many have left my mind. But there is Henri Briand, also Paul Fournet. Also our second-in-charge, Duclair. But Bernay, Bernay is the leader. His plans I am carrying out to the units. He also has charge of the wireless by which messages are exchanged with London.'

'And the place of meeting?'

'Is a cellar, the cellar of a small hotel. The hotel, the front, all have been closed by the Commandant of the town. But to the cellar there is good access, one may approach by several ways, and it is there that Bernay instals the wireless, with, for aerial, the lightning conductor of the hotel.'

'And the name of that hotel, monsieur?'

'Madame, I do not lie. It is then called the Hotel Bellevue, and stood upon the Rue Pasteur.'

Gabrielle's expression was blank, but I knew that Caudry had got it right. Traitor or no, there was little question of his involvement with that affair. Then I caught a flicked glance from him, a split-second of appraisal: weighing me up, seeking to judge if I were biting or not. I said:

'Let's get to cases. Did you take part in any actions?'

'But monsieur, yes. In many actions. I was not merely the messenger-boy. Only, monsieur, now it is known, such actions did very little harm, they being arranged with *les Chleuhs'* connivance to maintain Bernay's position. Thus, his own group are scatheless, not one member is arrested, while all around, perhaps as far as Rouen, arrests were happening right and left.'

'Bernay was shopping them.'

'Of course. And who is going to smell a rat? He works in the Mayor's office, where daily *les Chleuhs* are making visits. This accounts for our success, we think, because our clever leader keeps his eye on them. And we were right, yes? But for a very different reason.'

'And if this is now plain to you, Caudry, should it not also be plain to others?'

'He is clever to the end, monsieur. And none survived the group but I.'

'Then who would others suppose betrayed them?'

'They think perhaps just that the luck ran out.'

'Even though you, too, escaped the firing-squad?'

'Monsieur, until Wednesday, perhaps even Bernay did not know that.'

'And Bernay is dead.'

I had it then, that animal stare I had met before: molten, ferocious, but come and gone in a moment. For the briefest of intervals a different man was leaning there at the counter, surrounded by displays and by the odour of sheepskin garments.

Gabrielle had seen it too, was gazing at Caudry with a new attention: too late he'd slipped back into the obsequious shopkeeper with the cajoling, persuading smile.

Followed a silence broken only by the murmur of traffic, the shuffle of footsteps on the pavement: more deadly, it might be, than any questioning. And Caudry, it might be, was understanding it. At last Gabrielle exclaimed:

'So then let us hear of monsieur's escape – of how, when his comrades are surrounded and taken, he slips away with a song on his lips!'

'Oh madame, am I to blame for that, should I have asked them to shoot me too?'

'It would have been an act of integrity, monsieur, which the whole of France would have honoured. But not so, ha? Monsieur becomes invisible. From Trouville monsieur departs far away. And never again monsieur returns to this scene of his so-gallant exploits.'

'I am captured, imprisoned, madame!'

'Then why, like the others, were you not shot?'

'Because they do not make the connection, madame, it is the time of the invasion, all sixes and sevens.'

'On your papers, would it not say Trouville?'

'My papers, oh la! We had many papers.'

'So, also, monsieur, did the Gestapo. Did you run so far that you were out of their clutches?'

'Perhaps even yes – les Chleuhs are getting out, and the Gestapo are not the hindermost. They are burning their papers, commandeering transport, rushing to get back across the Rhine.'

'Clearly, monsieur, you are a survivor.'

'Like others, madame, by the bon chance.'

'By means known only to you. And to Monsieur Bernay.'

'Madame, my records are on file in this country.'

'Pah, your records!' Gabrielle turned to mime a spit. 'So now you will tell us, monsieur shopkeeper, of your amazing escape from les Chleuhs in Trouville.'

'Yes, I will tell you.'

Throughout this assault he had kept the fragile smile fluttering on his lips. Almost as though Gabrielle were a fractious customer whose unreasonable demands he was whittling away. Now he made a jesting pass at his brow: on which, however, was no sweat.

'It is D-Day, yes? We are long expecting it, our plans are made for the great moment. Yet even Bernay, it seems, is not advised when it will be. So, a surprise. We wake to gunfire, to many planes overhead, to *les Chleuhs* rushing about in panic and issuing fresh orders every minute. The Allies have landed in Normandy, where *les Chleuhs* do not expect them: this is our chance. Had we known before, perhaps not so many tanks rolling down the coast road! I deliver groceries, I deliver orders. And, that evening, we are summoned to the cellar.'

I said: 'By whom?'

'By whom, monsieur? Is not our leader Bernay? And am I not the group messenger who carries his orders, runs the errands?'

'On such a day you were delivering groceries?'

'Oh monsieur, the whole town is on the streets! It is the invasion, the Allies are coming, *les Chleuhs* have other things on their minds. Several times that day I call even at the Mayoralty, and who is there to take notice?'

'In the evening, wouldn't there have been a curfew?'

'In the evening it is the same. The Allies are coming, *les Chleuhs* are finished, no one heeds the curfew any more. And so it goes on. We have our summons. It is to be at the cellar at nine. But, the last thing, I have this message to a unit that could not be reached before.'

'A unit where?'

'At Touque, monsieur. Alas, they also were taken and shot.'

'That was very unfortunate.'

'Indeed yes. But my errand there was my salvation. As I approach the hotel, always cautious, I see that which makes me take instant cover. I throw myself down behind a derelict car, and, from there, can see all that happens.'

'What was it you saw that made you hide?'

61

'Soldiers, monsieur. In the hotel yard. And I am not long behind the old *Avant* when past sweeps a Mercedes, and into the yard.'

'You could see into the yard?'

'But yes. The car was placed there for that very purpose, to reconnoitre before approaching the cellar. You may be quite certain I had the yard in view.'

'Who was in the Mercedes?'

'Two Gestapo men and the town commandant, a General Schroeder. Also another man, who, at first, I cannot believe my eyes are seeing.'

'Go on.'

'Pierre Bernay.'

I stared long.

'He was under arrest?'

'No more than you or I, monsieur. He was there on a footing with the others. He is standing by them at a small distance, the Gestapo men and the General. One Gestapo man has a list, he shows it to Bernay, who nods and returns it. Then the General signals to his men and they throw back the doors and rush into the cellar. There is shooting. Two soldiers are wounded. One comrade is brought out, dead. The others, with guns thrust in their backs, and under the muzzles of guns without. They see Bernay. They see he is free. They see him with no gun thrust in his back. One, Laurent, seeks to throw himself on Bernay, but is shot at once and kicked aside. No questions, monsieur. No interrogation. What need, when Bernay can tell them all? They are lined up. I cannot watch more. But the shots are in my ears as I pedal away.'

I went on staring.

'You saw a great deal.'

'Monsieur, it is what I shall never forget.'

'There were lights in that yard?'

'It is June, and daylight till later still.'

'How near the yard were you?'

'Sixty, seventy metres. It is but from the corner and across the street.'

'And you stayed there to watch the whole scene played out?'

'I am transfixed. I cannot move.'

I shrugged. 'You were brave, monsieur. I would have made my escape a great deal earlier. In fact, when I first saw the soldiers and knew that my group had been betrayed. You were not transfixed later?'

'The horror spurs me, monsieur. To watch my comrades shot down I could not. It may be that monsieur has not suffered such experiences, cannot estimate truly their effect.'

I grunted. 'So now you're away. Suppose we hear how it goes from there.'

His lips weren't smiling for a moment. But he was quickly back in his stride.

'Monsieur, I am plainly on Bernay's list, whether or not they count the bodies. I cannot go back to my lodgings over the grocer's, nor remain any longer in Trouville. Westward the battle is raging, eastward my best hope. In such a city as Rouen, I am thinking, I may lie low, perhaps assisted by comrades. So I ride and I ride, keeping always to country ways, at times hearing the armour rush by in the distance, the droning of planes over my head. A long ride, a long night. I reach Rouen in great exhaustion. And, it is my luck, am at once picked up by *les Chleuhs*, who are rounding-up the able-bodied to labour in their factories in the Ruhr.'

I said: 'At this late stage, monsieur – with the invasion on their doorstep?'

'But yes, monsieur, so late they are still recruiting forced labour. I am, of course, in deadly fear that intelligence has come from Trouville, but no, no such intelligence, and I am shipped off to Gelsenkirchen. It may be true that they do not count the bodies, or require Bernay to identify them, and thus, when he enters this shop on Wednesday, at first he thinks he is staring at a ghost. However, I am not discovered. I am set to work filling shells. And in due course, monsieur, I am liberated, and found an occupation with the British Army, with whom, it is my good fortune, I remove to this fine country. Here, I take service with Monsieur Doughty, the former owner of this shop, and, in time, am married to his daughter, my late wife Marilyn.'

'And, to return no more to Trouville.'

'Alas, it would have wrung my heart.'

'Even though, seven miles down the road, ferries leave daily for Dieppe?'

'Oh, monsieur!' His whole body was in the shrug.

'So,' I said. 'In a moment of great personal danger, in the dull light of a late evening in June, at a distance, shall we say, of one hundred metres, you positively identify that man as Bernay?'

'Monsieur, who should know him better than I?'

'It was not a third member of the Gestapo who you saw?'

'Never. To my grave I will swear it. And please recall that he escaped the shooting.'

'Like yourself.'

'I explain that, monsieur.'

'But unlike yourself, to be hailed a hero.'

'Did I not say he was a man of great guile, who, until the very end, had deceived the comrades?'

I said: 'Caudry, when you told me this tale before there was no mention of seeing Bernay along with the Gestapo. In that version you had him manning the wireless, down in the cellar with the others.'

'Monsieur, I was greatly disturbed, I may by chance have given such an impression. I wished to convey my urgent danger, not relate every detail.'

'And that was a detail? That he arrived in their car? Checked their list? Watched the operation?'

'Perhaps, monsieur, even of such a dog, I was unwilling to tell these things.'

'Yet you tell them now.'

Again the great shrug.

I said: 'Monsieur, I am not satisfied. I must talk again with my friend from Evreux and have him check the facts of this story.'

'Monsieur – no!' In a moment he was grabbing my arm with a trembling hand. 'Do you not yet understand? In all these years, Bernay remains a hero with the comrades. Will my witness be believed? No, never! To them at the best, I am a vile slanderer. And as you are saying, there are daily ferries, but a few kilometres down the road. Would you put me in this danger, when, after all, the man is dead?'

'Is it such a grave danger?'

'Madame, tell your husband! I am good as dead. They will not ask questions, like you, monsieur. They will come with a rope and with a placard.'

'For speaking slander they will kill you?'

His fingers were drilling into my arm.

'Like you, they will remember that I escaped the shooting. And that here in a mortuary Bernay lies dead. These men do not ask questions, monsieur, and do not think they will not come. If you have pity, ring your friend from Evreux and tell him you misunderstood, and that the matter is explained.'

'But the matter isn't explained.'

'It is my life, monsieur!'

'On Thursday, it was the life of Monsieur Bernay.'

'God's finger was in that storm, monsieur. He judged between us, and chose Bernay.'

'A divine intervention.'

'Was it not so?'

'In my profession they find small favour.' I plucked my arm from his shuddering grip. 'Suppose we talk about Thursday evening. After you drove back here from London. Let's hear about your movements after that.'

He was back leaning against the counter, the mechanical smile long put to rest. And the staring eyes suddenly a mask behind which the real man had retired.

'You cannot think –?'

'Tell me.'

'I am here, monsieur. In my shop.'

'You didn't leave it?'

'But no. I am safest here, behind locked doors. Monsieur is aware that I am given protection, and, indeed, a police car twice passes by. They will tell you. I am here. Later, I am wakened by the terrible storm.'

'You were here at nine o'clock.'

'Certainly.'

'At ten o'clock.'

'But yes.'

'Then, if a witness saw you and your car elsewhere at that time, we are to take it that the witness was mistaken?'

In the depth of the eyes, a flicker.

'What witness is that?'

'Please answer the question.'

'Monsieur, my car, a Ford Sierra estate, is a vehicle not uncommon. It is a mistake that, in the hours of darkness, might very easily occur.'

'Though you were seen to be driving the car?'

Another flicker.

'Where, monsieur?'

'Perhaps on the approach to Seldon campsite?'

'Oh monsieur! Is that very likely?'

'Very likely, Caudry. Bernay was camped there, of which you seem to be aware, and we have testimony that a car was parked in the lane at around ten-fifteen that night. Fifteen minutes later the lights and radio in Bernay's van were switched off, and somebody very quietly closed the van door. This is witnessed. And we find that the cause of Bernay's death was a blow to the head.'

'But monsieur . . . a blow?'

I didn't reply. The staring eyes were quite blank again. Somewhere in there a lightning brain was reviewing, calculating. Then it came.

66

'In the first place, monsieur, I deny utterly what you are saying. No witness saw me or saw my car, which was all night secured in my yard at the back. But suppose it was so, suppose Bernay was murdered, suppose even that I was the guilty person, would it not be a case of self-defence against a person who threatens my life?'

'Was it you, Caudry?'

'Monsieur, I scorn your allegation. It is worthless. The police of this town will tell you I never left this shop.'

'Where perhaps you were writing sale-tickets?'

'Pardon?'

On the counter was a box of tissues. I took one and went to the display of camping odds and ends. There was only one of them, and it looked shop-soiled: a wooden peg-mallet with an iron-bound head; a head which, at a quick estimate, measured in diameter about seven centimetres. Using the tissue, I picked it up, held it out towards Caudry.

'The last of your stock?'

His eyes blazed out at me, but the thin lips were tight shut. I tore a bag from a bunch hanging beside the counter, slipped the mallet into it, scribbled on the bag.

'Do you wish for a receipt?'

He wouldn't answer, except for the venom in his eyes.

To Gabrielle, I said: 'Let's go,' and we went out of that shop, closing the door on the smell of sheepskin which, ever since, I have found nauseating.

5

We crossed the somnolent, sunny High Street, and then Gabrielle turned to look back at the shop. Caudry's grey face was staring after us over the notice that said Closed. We couldn't see his expression, just the gaunt, suspended face. For a moment. Then it seemed to dissolve into the shadows of the shop, where lights were switched off: like the face of a Cheshire Cat. Gabrielle drew a sudden, deep breath.

'That is a man I hope not to meet again.'

'You have made up your mind, then.'

'My mind, no. It is within *here* that I know him to be evil.'

Yes: within *there*. However good his story, however flimsy the evidence: about Caudry an aura, like the smell of the sheepskin.

'Without Bernay's testimony, it might be difficult to nail him down.'

'He lies, my friend. His story is false. I do not know where. But I can smell it.'

'It fitted what you knew?'

'He knew it must, and so he made sure that it did. I think perhaps you lay a finger on it and he invents what he saw in the hotel yard. He stay to watch? Ha! At the first sight of a uniform he is away. And now he invents a tale to inculpate poor Monsieur Bernay.'

'He could really believe that Bernay was the traitor.'

'And he would invent a tale to prove it? No, no, my friend. It is otherwise. Out of his fear comes that tale.'

'Which doesn't neccessarily prove he was the traitor himself.'

'If a traitor there was, then the traitor was Caudry.'

I shrugged, gazing back at the darkened shop. Yes, I was ready to believe it too. But belief cuts no ice in a court of law, and in my trade the proof is all.

'I must take this mallet to Ringmer.'

'But yes. And that perhaps will do the business?'

'It may.'

'I think, yes. And it is best before the comrades learn of this.'

We walked on, turned down by our hotel on the way to the police station, Gabrielle's arm in mine, our steps in time. But still the presence of Caudry dogged us, reaching after us from the shop in the High. Gabrielle said:

'I do not know. Perhaps forty years is too long a time. And the fear of that man is disgusting me. I might feel pity if I could.'

'You would forgive him?'

'Ha. No. But suddenly I wish I have not come here. With myself also I may be disgusted. We should leave these things to our men.'

'It may yet be a storm in a teacup – an accidental death, a man suffering from delusions.'

'You are right. And I will try to think so. Also that it is a sunny day.'

We came to the police station. Among the cars outside it, I spotted a white Renault 21. The car was a lefthand-drive model: and the plates on it were French plates.

'You wouldn't speak froggy, sir, would you?'

Ringmer's stolid face wore a look of desperation, and from down the passage we had heard the woman's voice storming away in demotic French. In fact there were two of them in the office, the other an apologetic-looking man; but he was being pushed into the background by his angry-faced companion. Short, stout, in her sixties, bursting out of a black gown, greying hair worn in a tight bun, she stood confronting Ringmer's desk. We were interrupting: she threw us a mean look, refused to give way. I said in French:

'I speak a little, and madame my wife is a French lady.'

'Ha – aha!' The woman swung round at once. 'Now perhaps we shall get some sense around here! Till this moment I am treated like a fool, and my brother, André, is worse than useless – *Anglais* he can speak, says he, but cannot even ask the way here.'

'Oh, Simone . . .!'

'Yes. Is true. And the ugly *gendarme* speaks no French. Then fetch an interpreter, I say, but can I get it through to his thick skull? Again and again I say it, but I talk to an organ-grinder's monkey.'

I said: 'You have business with the Leyhurst Police, madame?'

She drew herself up. 'Regard me, monsieur! I am the widow of a brave man who is killed in an accident, as I am told. Ha, ha, that is likely, yes, when he is Pierre Bernay, the hero of Trouville? But we shall see, we shall see, though the *Anglais* gendarmes are never so stupid.'

'You are Madame Bernay?'

'Does it not yet sink in?'

'Then, my profound condolences, madame. If I or my wife can be of assistance, we will be happy to oblige.'

'You are very genteel, monsieur. But are you not also of the gendarmes?'

'Oh, Simone!' her brother pleaded. 'These people but wish to help us.'

She made a nasal sound. 'Zhut! But I shall trust as I shall find.' Then she sniffed. 'His body is where? My poor Pierre, where have you laid him?'

I translated to Ringmer, who looked alarmed.

'She can't have him till after the inquest, sir. And maybe not then. I took that statement from the Streeters, and it does look as though we've got a case on our hands.'

'But she can see him?'

'He won't be pretty, sir. I'd sooner you headed her off.'

'May I mention that enquiries are proceeding?'

'Well – yes, sir. If you must.'

I translated the first part of the message, and at once Madame Bernay set up a wail.

'I will see him, yes? What do I care if his body is as you say? In the war I have seen such things, I am not afraid of dead bodies. And this is Pierre, my own Pierre, bereft of his life in a foreign land. Also, how shall you know it is he, unless his own wife clasps the body in her arms?'

I didn't answer that one.

'She still wants to see him.'

Ringmer made a face. 'Very well, sir.'

He rose, and led the way to the small morgue at the rear of the building. I, too, was interested to see Bernay, and thankfully Praed had left him tidy: the sheet was turned back from a turbanned head and features more or less composed. An ascetic face with the shred of grey beard and the nose made prominent by death. A strong brow, cheekbones. Teeth, pupils, just visible. Empty-faced, Madame Bernay gazed down at him. Then, with a cry, threw herself on the body.

'Pierre. Oh Pierre.'

It was Gabrielle who laid a hand on her shoulder.

'Madame.'

'Oh Pierre!'

Gently, Gabrielle drew her back from the body.

'Oh madame, you cannot know.' She clutched Gabrielle to her. 'Before he leaves we have words, I did not wish him to make this trip. In the morning he leaves with no break-fast – I have not made him one last coffee! And with this picture in his heart he dies. Oh madame, I am a desolate woman!'

'It is nothing, madame. He would have forgiven you.'

'I would not watch him drive away.'

71

'These are smaller matters. He would not doubt you loved him.'

'It is I, not he, who should be lying there.'

Weeping, she allowed herself to be led away, down the long corridor back to the office. Her brother hovered round her, helped her to a chair. Ringmer hastily ordered a brew-up of tea.

'Oh my Pierre. My little one.'

And it didn't sound absurd.

'But why had he not shaved . . .?'

The bristle is emphasized on the face of a corpse.

A mug was thrust in her hand: she drank, then spat tea on Ringmer's lino.

'Is it not enough, but you must poison me?'

'Oh, Simone!' her brother chided.

Madame Bernay wiped her mouth, slowly rose from the chair. She fixed her stabbing black eyes on Ringmer, who shrank a little from their gaze.

'Translate what I say to this *gendarme*! Accident? Pouf! No accident here. By the hand of an assassin died my Pierre, and that assassin I shall name.'

I translated.

'Oh lord!' Ringmer gaped. 'She can't have got on to Caudry already.'

I said: 'Madame?'

'You will tell him this. I name Gustave Darlan, the betrayer of Trouville. Who was thought dead. But who yet lives. And who is a citizen of this town.'

'. . . Gustave Darlan?'

'Please to translate.'

But Ringmer had got the message already. He was goggling, shaking his head; at last gave a helpless shrug.

'Tell her we know of no such man.'

I told her.

'But yes. That man is here!'

'The name is unknown in Leyhurst, madame.'

'Then, by another name he goes.'

'You have reason to believe that he is here?'

'A better reason who can have? The word of my husband, who here has seen him, and, because of this, lies now on a slab.'

'You had a communication with your husband?'

'Alas no. It is with my brother. André, relate to monsieur the call you had from my Pierre.'

The brother dithered: a neat, small-featured man, some years older than Madame Bernay.

'It is on Wednesday evening, monsieur, that I receive a telephone call from Pierre. It is to tell me that he has met this Frenchman who so closely resembles Gustave Darlan.'

'Resembles?'

'He cannot be certain after a time so long. He said he would observe this man, to make more sure that it was he.'

'Did he say where he met him?'

'But yes. It is in some shop where Pierre goes. More he will not tell me in case, after all, it is an innocent man. Monsieur must understand that Gustave Darlan is a name reviled throughout Normandy, and merely to suspect that a man was he would be a terrible thing for that man.'

'Do you have this man's description?'

'Alas no. His comrades were slaughtered, and a few who remembered him say only he was tall and shifty-eyed. Alone, Pierre had the picture in his brain, might see those eyes and know he looked on Darlan.'

'But he wasn't certain.'

'Monsieur.'

'He is certain, he is certain!' Madame Bernay broke in. 'Oh yes. I know my Pierre. About this matter he shall be very cautious, but he is certain, or why ring at all? Darlan is here, and who shall hide him? Tall, shifty-eyed and French. A man who shall be nearing seventy, and living for many years in this country.'

'Such a man might still not be Darlan, madame.'

'You tell me this? Is Pierre not dead?'

'Your husband's van was crushed by a tree.'

'Zhut! And you fools would look no further?'

'Hush, Simone!' her brother pleaded.

But Madame Bernay's eyes were popping at mine.

'This once you listen, yes, you attend to the widow of a dead hero? Darlan is here. After all these years, he meets face to face with the man he most fears, he sees the look in that man's eyes, knows himself at last discovered. Monsieur, monsieur, he is looking at his fate. Never will the comrades cease to hunt him. He must silence this man, this deadly witness, or never sleep again at night. The tree crushes the van, yes. But within that van lay a dead body.'

'Madame, so far this is inference – '

'Monsieur, Darlan shall be smoked out.'

'If, indeed, there has been a crime, rest assured that we will punish the perpetrator.'

'Then you had best work fast, monsieur. Because the comrades may work yet faster.'

And in the black eyes was a glitter that, for a moment, recalled Caudry.

'Madame,' Gabrielle said. 'Is it then so certain this man was the traitor? I am from Rouen, madame, and have heard of the betrayal, but until now not of Gustave Darlan.'

Madame Bernay eyed her.

'You have not heard of Darlan, or of the witness that my husband bore?'

'What witness, madame?'

Madame Bernay spat. 'On the night of D-Day, madame, in the courtyard of the Bellevue Hotel, just before the comrades were taken out and shot. Himself in peril, Pierre saw Darlan in the company of two Gestapo agents.'

'He saw – Darlan?'

'From behind an old car, where he had taken cover after catching sight of the soldiers.'

Ringmer tried to interrupt, but I waved him down – time to bring him up-to-date later! Here we had it, at only secondhand, the version that Bernay could no longer tell us. If a clever invention, as Caudry claimed, or something closer to the facts – no matter: we needed to hear it. I waved Ringmer to silence.

'Madame,' Gabrielle said. 'I have heard such a tale before. But was not your husband the leader of the group, which was so famous for its exploits?'

'The leader, madame? Ha! You have heard fairy-tales in Rouen. My husband is then a young man of eighteen, how shall such a youth lead the group?'

'A young man of eighteen?'

'I am saying. And younger still when he joined the comrades. He is from Pont l'Eveque, madame, where his family yet reside, and at that time he is apprenticed to a butcher in Trouville. Such a person is useful to the comrades, under the noses of *les Chleuhs* he may go his errands. The group, the unit depend on Pierre, and never once does he fail to get through.'

'Then, madame, who was the leader?'

'Who else, but that vile Gustave Darlan? It is a Gestapo plot from the beginning, madame, a plot to infiltrate the whole area. They will set up a puppet group, yes, a group to have contacts throughout the region, a group with wireless, a group whose exploits shall be successful and celebrated. Oh, it is clever. And for two long years the manipulation is unsuspected. There are arrests and torturings and shootings, and an iron cross, doubtless, for the Gestapo commandant.'

'The exploits of this group were manoeuvred?'

'That was essential to the plot, madame, though, since the comrades were acting in good faith, not always to the satisfaction of *les Chleuhs*. There were improvisations.

75

Pierre has told me. A little harmless derailment becomes a major disaster. But these *les Chleuhs* have to swallow, and they increase the group's reputation.'

'A strange story, madame.'

'Ha.'

'And never was this man, Darlan, suspected?'

'Who shall suspect him? His record is success, no plan of Darlan's ever fails. And why? The reason seems plain. He is an employee in the Town Hall. There also the town's commandant had made his headquarters, and *les Chleuhs'* movements are an open book to Darlan.'

'None witnessed his conferences with *les Chleuhs*?'

'You may depend upon that, madame.'

'So your husband was the single witness of his guilt.'

'He, alone, escaped to denounce the traitor.'

Gabrielle said flatly: 'That was fortunate, madame.'

The black eyes flashed. 'Dare you call him a liar?'

'I am wondering, madame, if he was not mistaken, at such a moment of danger and dismay as you describe.'

Madame Bernay spat. 'Such doubts, madame, are best not spoken where his friends may hear them. Oh no. There is no mistake. Darlan is the man standing there in the courtyard. And by chance only that poor Pierre is not added also to the martyrs of Trouville.'

'What, indeed, did he see?'

'The soldiers, madame, also four men getting out of a car. Two of these are Gestapo agents, and, out after them, steps Darlan. Pierre is stunned, he cannot believe. With these men, Darlan confers. One has a paper. Darlan examines it, then nods and hands it back to the man. Then the cellar is rushed. Pierre waits no more. Behind him is shooting, but not at him. He escapes, he gets clear of the town, he heads for Evreux, where he also has relatives. And there the comrades hide him in our woodshed, which, madame, was how I met Pierre Bernay.'

'This, too, I can vouch for,' put in the brother. 'I hear the tale from his lips in that very woodshed. The

76

poor fellow is badly shaken up and can barely stammer through his tears. Quickly comes the news that confirms his story – the entire group at Trouville arrested and shot. At once the comrades are hunting for Darlan, but – aha – no Darlan.'

'Because why?' Madame Bernay spat. 'Because, madame and monsieur, because *les Chleuhs* have spirited him away to a place of safety, outside France. He is not among the bodies, no, they were left where they fell, each is accounted for. And never again is he seen in Trouville. Never again in *La belle France*. So, all this time, where is Darlan? What dirty corner does he infect? Monsieur, madame, in this town he has waited to finish the job he began in Trouville.'

I shook my head. 'That is still unproven.'

'Monsieur, I demand justice for the death of my husband.'

'The case will be investigated urgently, madame. Until then I must counsel you to stay patient.'

'Also, I am claiming my husband's body.'

'I regret, but that must wait until after the inquest.'

'Then there is nothing done – all shall be covered over – and still this man will walk on earth!'

'Oh, Simone!' the brother wailed.

'I will not be silenced, brother of mine. Have I not just clasped my husband's body, and am I now to be counselled to patience?' She stared up into my eyes. 'Monsieur, tell the monkey I *will* have justice. Either he attends to the matter himself, or among us are those who shall.'

I stared back at her. 'Madame, perhaps I can appreciate your feelings. But if you continue in these sentiments you may be arrested and sent back to France. Is that understood?'

And we stared very long.

'Oh, Simone, come away!' the brother groaned. 'We can do no more now, let us go and seek a lodging.'

'Very good, monsieur,' Madame Bernay said. 'I think perhaps you too are understanding. So, for this time, we will go. But tell the monkey that we shall be back.'

I bowed slightly.

'Madame.'

'Madame.'

Impatiently, the brother grabbed her arm. He was still holding it when, through the window, we saw them going to the white Renault.

'So, what the devil was that all about?'

I took time out to light my pipe. Only after the second match did I reply:

'We've just heard a story told two ways.'

'Two ways?' Ringmer echoed.

'We came here straight from our chat with Caudry.'

I filled him in. He listened frowningly. I didn't try to tilt the scales: two accounts of an incident, nearly identical. Just the one important difference. At the end his frown was even deeper.

'So Moossoo wasn't giving us a line! And now we've got Bernay's wife on our backs, threatening what she will do.'

'More or less.'

'Are we believing her?'

'The point is she's believing in herself. Her and her friends in France. The truth is forty years ago.'

'But Christ . . . if it is true . . .'

'Oh, it is true!' Gabrielle exclaimed. 'That man in the shop is knowing too much about what happened at the arrests. Oh yes. That is his mistake. He puts in details he should not have known.'

'And that's your opinion, sir?'

I puffed. 'About.'

'But that's handing Moossoo a fat motive, sir. I mean, before it was just one of his tales, but with this, and the Streeters' statement and all . . .'

78

'And this.'

I laid on his desk the bag I'd been carrying all this while.

Ringmer opened it cautiously, peered inside, pulled the bag open some more to expose the mallet-head. His eyes rounded.

'You got this from Moossoo?'

'From a sell-off display in the shop. Note that it isn't exactly mint. And has the appearance of grease on the face.'

'And the size is right, sir.'

'It fits.'

Ringmer kept gazing. 'Then we've got him.'

I shook my head. 'Not yet. Not without a positive report from the lab. Just now Caudry is denying everything and we can't tie him to events at the campsite. He swears he never left his premises, and that your patrols can prove it.'

'My patrols!'

'Didn't they keep an eye on him?'

'Well yes, sir – more or less. But we weren't taking his old buck seriously, and I daresay they only looked in once or twice.'

'The critical time was between ten and eleven.'

'Which was when the pubs were turning out. I'll have a word with them, but it's odds-on that they weren't around Moossoo's at just that time.'

'Just one sighting of his car would help.'

'Leave it to me, sir,' Ringmer said.

'And this to forensic right away.'

'Right away, sir.' He reached for the phone.

The mallet was dispatched.

Ringmer said: 'I don't know, sir, but I'm not feeling easy about this one. If all that froggy malarkey is true, we could have something comic blowing up here.'

'So, the quicker you act the better.'

'Perhaps we should pull him in. For his own protection.'

'I read the riot act to the lady,' I said. 'And I don't think her brother is looking for trouble.'

'They're almost bound to spot him, sir.'

I shrugged: it would be a miracle if they didn't! 'Put a man outside the shop. But you'll need that report before you feel his collar.'

Still Ringmer was looking unhappy. 'I'm finding it hard to take this lot in, sir,' he said. 'I mean, I've known Moossoo since I was a kid. He's always been a bit of a curio, but this is like someone turned over a stone. I can't believe it.'

'There's small room for doubt.'

'But it's a shaker, all the same. Like waking up one morning to find the milkman is Jack the Ripper.'

'Just get them to hurry up the report,' I said.

'Yes sir. But it's a queer old world.'

We left him to it.

Gabrielle murmured: 'That poor policeman is too English. But Madame Bernay, ha-ha. I think she will not give up so soon.'

'Caudry should be arrested some time today.'

'And that is best for all, my friend.'

To regain the hotel we had to pass near the shop, still dark and exhibiting the notice: Closed. It appeared deserted: no face peered out at us, no movement within betrayed Caudry's presence. Above, the windows of his flat were tight shut, and not a tremor in the net curtains. A low profile; and that he'd better keep.

Because a white Renault was sitting in the hotel carpark.

6

We took our very late lunch alone, a snack meal in a corner of the lounge. Before we went to it I checked the register, and yes, Madame Bernay and her brother had booked in. Were they given a front room? I enquired. Happily, no: two singles at the back, overlooking the carpark. They had booked in and then gone out: doubtless to begin their hunt for Caudry. Lunch was thoughtful. We had the shop in view across the traffic-busy street, and it was not long before an unmarked Escort crept slowly to a parking in a slot opposite. The driver, a fair-haired young man, eased his seat back and unfolded a newspaper. But he wasn't reading it. A few minutes later, he lit a cigarette, blew smoke boredly. I drew Gabrielle's attention to him.

'Ringmer's watchdog.'

But for the moment he had little to watch. We saw a customer or two try the door, stare at the notice, and pass on. Had our French couple done the same? Bernay, it appeared, had not identified the shop, and Caudry had only to keep his head down to avoid their attention. Anyway, we saw nothing of them as we ate our lunch in the lounge of The Swinburne.

We drank our coffee. Gabrielle said:

'My dear, I am fatigued with this wretched affair. That man is haunting me. I wish I had not met him. I wish I was reading about this in a newspaper.'

'I'm sorry you saw what you did at the police station.'

'The poor lady also, that was no joke. But it is the man who I cannot get my mind from, the man who is cringing in his fear across there. This, then, is what it is to be a traitor, to be the betrayer of one's comrades, this is the end of it. The man over there. Hiding his face from human sight.'

'It will be over soon.'

'It cannot be over. What is done cannot be undone. You may put him in prison, aha, but can that change what he is? His ears have heard the echo of gunfire in a courtyard in Trouville, the curses of the betrayed. He knows himself beyond pity.'

'At least his fear is understandable.'

'His fear also is gross, is obscene. I could wish to leave this town, now, and return to our cold, dark flat. May we not do that?'

'Well . . . yes.'

'But, you wish to see this matter out?'

I nodded. Yes, I did. Though it wasn't my business, still, I wanted to see it tied up.

'Then, so be it, my friend. But there is little more for you to do. The man is under guard, and the good Inspector Ringmer has the affair in his hands. Thus, though we remain in this place, we are free to do as we please. Let us, therefore, drive our car to a place that may be more cheerful.'

'To a place . . .?'

'Are we not near the coast? I desire a breath of air from the sea, perhaps from France. We shall do this?'

'Well . . .'

'Then finish your coffee, my friend.'

I drank with some reluctance. She was probably right, and my presence there of small utility; at the same time I wanted to be around when that report came in from forensic, and to be present, if the truth were known, when Ringmer made the pinch. Not my case, but I'd set it up, didn't want to see it fumbled. And there was the factor of Madame Bernay *et frère* combing shops along the High . . .

82

'A short trip, then. To the coast.'

'My dear man. Who is kind.'

I hung on to light my pipe. The shop across the way stayed as lifeless as ever, and, staring at it, I was imagining again the smell of sheepskin in my nostrils.

We drove south, with the smooth line of the Downs riding behind us, skirted Southhaven, headed for the level brow of Bawdsey head. And we had it alone; it may have been that the storm had swept such excursions from people's minds; in delicate sunlight we parked on the turf, with the Channel, still disturbed, an apron of grey below us. We approached the edge till we could see the beach and the bearded rollers breaking. Gulls were squealing far beneath; some wreckage bobbed on the breakers. Southward the Channel was lost in haze and there a ghostly ship was suspended.

'This breeze, it comes perhaps from Normandy?'

I thought it probably had too much west in it.

'And it is from that port, on a fateful day, that you set sail for Dieppe?'

Gabrielle had never used the ferry; her trips to France were made from Heathrow. Now she was staring at the sea wistfully, hands clasped, feet planted.

'You are feeling homesick?'

'Aha. It is, perhaps, those people. I do not know. But of a sudden I have this longing to be over there.'

'A flying visit might be possible. There is probably an afternoon sailing.'

She was silent a moment, then shook her head. 'It is just a foolish yearning, my friend.'

'That ship we can see out there may be the morning sailing from Dieppe.'

We watched its snail-like progress out of the haze that hid all else, the tall, white superstructure, the black hull with its indecipherable letterings. Out of France. Out of Normandy. Rolling a little as she came. Lightly-loaded no doubt, because how many would be travelling on that day? How many . . .?

Gabrielle said: 'It may be I am feeling a little ashamed for France. That such a man as that one is French, and, what is worse, of Normandy. I am humbled by that man, my friend. I feel I am reduced in your eyes.'

'That's nonsense, of course.'

'Indeed, but I feel it. I would rage and threaten like Madame Bernay. For what can one do about such a creature? Even the rope and lamp-post are not enough.'

'You would never be party to such an act.'

'You say? It may be true. But oh, I can understand those who would, and the despair in their hearts that would drive them.'

'The despair . . .?'

'*Oui*. You must guard that man when you have him, George. For it will not end there. Once these things are known, sooner or later, the Resistance will come. Bernay gave warning before he died, and madame his wife will not stay silent.'

'He will be held in a high-security prison.'

'So have been others. But justice was done.'

I drew on an empty pipe. Now the ferry was standing proud from the haze. One could see from her fluctuating bow-wave that the roll was not inconsiderable. Within half-an-hour, at most, she would be nosing into the harbour at Southhaven, edging up to the ramp, opening her doors, letting her cargo of vehicles stream out. Trucks, cars, laden at Dieppe. Out of France. Out of Normandy.

'Shall we go down and watch her dock?'

Gabrielle slowly nodded. 'It may do me good. My dear, just now I am very bad company, and that sin too I lay at his door.'

We got back in the Rover and drove. Ten minutes brought us to the ferry terminal. The ship, a French boat, was already in the river when I parked by the AA port

84

office; I left Gabrielle in the car and strolled across to the customs sheds. I showed my warrant.

'Were there any sailings yesterday?'

The uniform-man did a double-take. 'You have to be joking, sir. One of the ferries broke loose and grounded on the beach. Nor you wouldn't have wanted to be out there either, the sort of seas we were getting.'

'What about today?'

'Two in and two out. That's the other one docking now. And if it's like the morning boat there won't be much getting off it.'

'Many Continentals this morning?'

He held up one hand. 'That's about it.'

'Was one of them a white Renault 21 driven by an elderly man with a plump lady passenger?'

He stared. 'That's right, sir. Came through the Green and asked the way to Leyhurst. Leastways I think they did, but my froggie was as bad as their anglais. They didn't look like villains, sir.'

'They weren't. Any others who caught your eye?'

'No sir. Just the usual lot coming over on the cheap fares.'

I left him looking after me thoughtfully – what was brass from the Yard doing asking these questions? – and strolled back to Gabrielle , who was gazing glumly at the manoeuvring ferry. Slowly, by feet, by inches, the towering vessel was joining up with the land: reducing, it seemed, in scale, the installations, the houses of the small town. A few tiny passengers watched from the rails, a few tiny men did their jobs on the quay: then the vessel was secure, appeared to have no further reason for its still-closed doors and raised ramp. Yet there was a pause, as though it drew breath at the completion of its journey.

'We are not just sight-seeing?'

Gabrielle knew.

'Madame Bernay was on the boat this morning.'

'And now we watch, yes, to see who it is that is coming this time.'

'It can do no harm.'

'My friend, you won't stop them. Today, tomorrow or next week. And meanwhile we are looking at the ship on which poor Monsieur Bernay perhaps planned to return home.'

I took her hand.

'We can drive back to town.'

She shook her head stubbornly. 'Not yet. With you, this matter is professional, my dear, but not so with me. I shall see it out.'

'Two days ago you knew none of these people.'

But she merely squeezed my hand.

The doors parted at last, the ramp descended, and at once vehicles began to emerge: trucks mostly, with just a sprinkling of cars, heading for the Green channel. Then, one by one, they began reappearing, mostly to park while they got their bearings. Citroens, Renaults, Peugeots. Young couples. Some with children. All looking pale and strained, the children wailing, some being sick. Maps were brandished, signs pointed to; then, uncertainly, the cars would move on. The cheap-fare brigade, nothing comic; come for a brief whiff of *Anglais*. But then:

'See! These are different.'

And Gabrielle squeezed my hand hard. A blue Citroen BX had come to park a short distance away, by the AA office. The same brandishing of maps, the same pointing; but this time the car contained four men. And they were not young men. The driver had black hair, but the others were greying: a bald patch gleamed. Clearly they were arguing about the route, one pointing one way, one another; then the map would change hands, and the argument begin afresh.

'Stay here, my friend.' Gabrielle's eyes gleamed. 'I will assist my poor fellow-countrymen.'

Then, before I could object, she had jumped out of the car and run over to the Citroen. The driver lowered his window; something she said; at once the *entente* was *cordiale*; eagerly, the map was handed through the window, and four heads craned towards it, hanging on her word. Gabrielle smoothed the map, traced a line on it, indicated the road through the town. Then she rattled off a couple of smiling questions, still holding the map in her hand, finally returning it to the black-haired driver and receiving a chorus of compliments and thanks. She gaily waved them away on the road she had indicated. But the gaiety had gone when she returned to the Rover.

'Well?'

'I do not know. It may well be as they say.'

'What did they say?'

'That they have come over to shop in London. But, it is a certain road they are wanting, the road that will take them through Leyhurst. They do not especially mention this town, but it is to this road they require directing.'

'Perhaps someone told them it was the best road.'

'Also this I can tell you. They are men all in their sixties. That driver dyes his hair.'

'Anything else?'

'Ha, yes. They are so ready to explain where they go. – You will be staying in these parts? I ask them. – Oh no, they say together, we are shopping in London. It is like a learnt lesson, my friend, all ready prepared for those who ask.'

I shrugged: they hadn't looked desperados, more like a party of jovial friends. But Gabrielle sat broodingly silent as we watched the rest of the intake through, and certainly those men were to be the only prospects; the last-comers seemed as innocent as the first. Finally she stirred.

'We go back to our hotel, now?'

'When we get back I shall call on Ringmer.'

'The arrest will be made?'

'I think it likely.'

She shivered very slightly as I started the car.

'My dear, you will drop me first. I find I cannot face seeing that man again. You will say your Gabrielle becomes a coward, but so it must be. I wish not to see him.'

'If he is arrested, he'll be in a cell.'

'It is the same. I wish not to be there. I will wait in the hotel for the news that you bring me.'

'We can still drive straight back to London.'

'No. Let it be as I say.'

And no more was said on the short drive back to our spot on the hotel park, where Gabrielle kissed me with unusual warmth before running in the back way, from which one couldn't see the shop. I went to stare at it, however. In the gathering dusk it looked darker than ever. But the Escort was still in position. Which meant that Ringmer hadn't made the pinch yet.

'Sir, the Chief Constable is here, and he's anxious to have a word with you.'

'Where do I find him?'

'He's with the Chief Inspector, sir. They've been trying to get you at the hotel.'

Well, Chief Constables I have known, including one who calls me George. Also in the office I found Ringmer's side-kick, a Detective Inspector Malling. The C.C., a dapper, moustached man, rose and held out a hand as I entered; he was manning the desk, with the others flanking him; Malling reluctantly yielded me his chair. The C.C.'s grasp was firm.

'Ah ... Gently. I'm damned glad you're still here. As though we didn't have enough on our plates, there's something odd going on with this Bernay business. You know the French a bit, don't you?'

I stared. 'I have French acquaintances.'

'A bit more than that, isn't it? I mean – I've been telling Ringmer – that run in with terrorists at Honfleur. You were in with the French police, their secret service, that sort of thing?'

'I met certain officers.'

'That's it. So perhaps you've an inkling of what's going on now. I've just had a ring – from Paris, mark you – from a certain Monsieur . . . I think the name was Hilaire. Know him, would you?'

I shook my head.

'Says he represents the *Direction de la* something.'

'The *Direction de la Surveillance du Territoire.*'

'There you are, I was sure you could tell me. French secret service, isn't it?'

'The equivalent of M.I.'s 5 and 6.'

'Exactly. The close-mouthed lot. And he was doing his top about Bernay. Said we should check, double-check what had happened, because the odds were there had been foul play, and that if a Frenchman chanced to be implicated they would wish to send a man to interrogate him. Hold on, I said, hold on, shouldn't this go through official channels? Then he got excited, like the French do, said we had to play this one close to our chests, top people involved and all that, fewest who know about it the better. Well, I mean, what's it about? Where am I supposed to go from here? Because it looks like there will be a Frenchman involved, with this damned Resistance angle on top.'

He stared with aggrieved eyes. I said:

'It could be one and the same thing.'

'How's that?'

'If Caudry is who we think, he may have some interesting information.'

'You mean about top frogs?'

'That could be possible. Involvements he knew about during the Occupation. Information the D.S.T could make use of. And which they certainly wouldn't want broadcast.'

'Like the Kurt Waldheim thing.'

'Like that.'

The C.C. shaped his lips in a whistle. 'I don't like it,' he said. 'It's getting in deep. And how sure are we our frog is the man they think?'

'Pretty sure.'

'Then why haven't we arrested him?'

'We haven't had the OK yet, sir,' Ringmer said. 'They lost power at the lab this afternoon, but we should get their report any moment now.'

'Can't you pull him in on spec?'

'Be risky, sir. That mallet's all we've got that can tie him in. I've had men chasing up sightings of his car, but they haven't turned in anything yet.'

'What about motive?'

'Well . . . there's that, sir.'

I said: 'To prove motive, we'll need to prove identity. The records will show he's a Jean Caudry, and the odds are we shall never prove different.'

The C.C. made frustrated noises. 'There's Bernay's widow – she doesn't seem to have many doubts. Engineer a confrontation, eh? See how the fellow stands up to that.'

Ringmer looked alarmed. 'She'd never met Darlan, sir.'

'Widow of the dead man. It might just floor him.'

'Be best if we could face him with the mallet, sir.'

'So where's the number of our damned laboratory?'

He rang forensic; he talked to them severely. Then he listened for a while. He looked a little happier. He rang off with a stern admonishment for them to ring him back soon, or sooner. He looked at us.

'We've got him.'

'Sir?'

'They're matching the grease on the face of the mallet. A French pomade, they think, and looks a ringer for the grease on Bernay's hair. Ninety percent certain. They're conducting the final test now.'

'Did they mention dabs, sir?'

'Those too. A bit smudged, but they've got some.'

Ringmer said: 'Looks like game, set and match.'

90

'Yes, game, set and match,' the C.C. said. But then the happy glint left his eye. 'Only there's still this fellow in Paris. I've never met this sort of carry-on before, and I'm hanged if I know how I should handle it.' He looked at me. 'Should I kick it upstairs?'

I said: 'It might just get the wrong sort of attention.'

'How's that?'

'Certain elements. Who might have a different use for Caudry's information.'

He stared hard and long.

'So what's the drill?'

'Unofficially,' I said. 'Forget it. But for that and several other reasons, keep Caudry in a place of maximum security.'

He stared some more. 'You really think they'd get at him?'

'Yes. I think they might try.'

'This Paris bunch?'

'And the comrades. If Caudry is Darlan, they'll never rest.'

'And that damned woman. We can't gag her.'

I shook my head: 'No.'

He brought his hands down on the desk. 'But, good lord, Gently, this is Sussex! Capers like this just don't go on here, not in my patch, not in Leyhurst. A bit of villainy here and there, we're no more perfect than the rest, but can you seriously tell me that, for forty odd years, we've been harbouring a war criminal in our High Street? It doesn't make sense. As far as I'm concerned this is a case of simple homicide, fellow gone off his rocker maybe, probably finish up in Broadmoor. Can't we leave it there?'

I shrugged. 'As long as our security stays intact.'

'That's my pigeon – '

The phone clanged, and he caught it first ring; listened, slammed it down, remained an instant with his hand on it.

'The lab, sir?' Ringmer ventured.

It was the lab.

'What are we waiting for?' the C.C. demanded.

I rode in the C.C.'s Merc the short distance from the police station to the High. Now the street-lights were lit, though an after-glow lay still on the Downs. We parked bang outside the shop, with the hotel windows bright across the way; with my eye I counted to our bedroom window, but it was dark, Gabrielle was elsewhere. Behind us, Ringmer parked, with Malling and two uniform-men in tow. The watchdog across the way had spotted us: he slid out of the Escort and came over.

'Anything to report?'

'Nothing, sir. He hasn't stirred while I've been here.'

'Did Bernay's widow show up?'

'Yes sir. Her and her brother. They peered into the shop and rattled the door, then they had a confab in froggie. But they didn't stay long, and I couldn't tell if they knew it was Moossoo's place.'

'Anyone else?'

'Just customers. Some of them swore when they found he was closed.'

'Where is Madame Bernay now?'

'I last saw her going back into the hotel.'

He was dispatched to guard the rear, while the C.C. marched up to the door and performed with the handle. Then he peered through his hands, trying to surprise some movement within. But the empty shop stayed empty, lit very faintly by one of the street-lamps; and the windows above stayed dark, stayed shut, the curtains motionless.

'Fellow's lying low . . . what's at the back?'

'A walled yard, sir,' Ringmer said. 'And a garage where he keeps his car.'

'One of you stay here. The rest come with me.'

We followed him into the lane that flanked the premises, where the watchdog was standing beside locked double-doors in a wall. Above it one could see windows at the back

92

equally dark with those at the front. The C.C. shouldered the doors experimentally, but they were clearly very solid doors. He stared meanly at the windows, then:

'Open up, there! This is the police.'

Nobody opened; he tried again. Nobody opened that time, either.

'We'll have to break in, sir,' Ringmer murmured.

'But damn it – is the fellow there at all?'

'Oh, he'll be in there, sir,' Ringmer said. 'I've had a car outside here since two, and the Chief Super was with him before that.'

'I left him shortly after one,' I said.

'I know, sir. But what else was there for him to do? He was scared stiff that his froggy pals would come looking for him, and the safest thing was to batten down hatches.'

The C.C. kept staring up at the darkened building.

'I don't like it,' he said. 'I don't like it at all. If he was as scared as everyone's saying – well, you know how unstable these frogs can be.'

Ringmer sucked air through his teeth. 'Not Moossoo,' he said.

'Push them hard enough,' the C.C. said. 'Look, just get these damned doors open, heaven knows what we're going to find inside.'

Malling produced a bunch of keys and a little jiggling did the trick; we entered a small yard encumbered with packing-cases and giving access to the rear door of the premises. The C.C. thundered on it.

'Open up, open up!'

Still the darkness, the silence prevailed. Malling jiggled again, the door succumbed, and we were stumbling over cartons and boxes in an atmosphere of sheepskin.

'Caudry – this is the police!'

Someone found a light-switch to reveal the storeroom we'd blundered into; also a flight of stairs that led to the flat above.

'Up there – two of you.'

Malling and a uniform-man obliged. The C.C. pressed on into the shop, and lights were beginning to blaze everywhere.

'He isn't up here, sir.'

'Then where the devil . . .?'

But already I was backing out into the yard. I tried the garage doors. The garage doors were unlocked. I found a switch inside: no car.

'He's away.'

'What – ?'

'He must have taken off after I left him.'

'But . . .!'

They came to gaze at the vacant place I had uncovered. A small garage, lined with clutter, a few oilstains on the concrete floor, but definitely no car. Not even of any kind.

'But then . . . the bastard's been gone for hours. He could be anywhere now.'

'Here's a cock-up!' the C.C. snarled. 'Where do we look for the so-and-so, hey?'

'Just a thought,' I said. 'France is unlikely, but there's a ferry-port down the road.'

'The ferry – yes.'

'There's a sailing this evening.'

'Good God – let me get my hands on a phone.'

The C.C. plunged back into the shop, closely attended by the dismayed Ringmer. But it was a long-shot. Caudry/Darlan would be panicking indeed if he sought escape across the Channel. London was a better bet. And he could have been there hours ago. On the heels of the call to the dock police at Southhaven should come another for a countrywide alert. I followed into the shop, now lit like a Christmas-tree, to put in my two-pennorth. But it wasn't necessary. The C.C. was already barking the order down the phone.

'I feel such a bloody fool, letting that fellow slip through my fingers. I mean, with an open-and-shut case like that.

94

And all this Comic Cuts stuff too.' The C.C. took a sniff of sheepskin. 'I suppose there's no chance of getting a line on him?'

'Well, there you are, sir – '

'I mean, wife's relatives, second home, something of that sort.'

'He was a loner, sir – '

'Bit of property somewhere.'

Ringmer could but shake his head. 'Of course, we'll search the premises for any clue, sir, but knowing Moossoo the way I do . . .'

The C.C. glared at me. 'Any comment, Gently?'

But I had nothing for the moment to add. With the police, comrades, French intelligence hot on his trail, Caudry was away and into the blue. Well, he'd proved himself a survivor. One almost felt an ashamed admiration.

'I feel such an arse,' the C.C. reiterated. 'But I suppose I should thank you for nailing him in the first place.'

It sounded like a pay-off line.

Outside in the street, a handful of gapers was already collecting.

7

The C.C. and his Merc departed, but I remained to assist in the search of the premises – less, perhaps, from a desire to be useful than from a curiosity about the man who had lived there.

His wife had died five years ago, according to Ringmer, and his father-in-law seven years before that. There was a sister-in-law, address unknown, but she had ceased to visit Caudry after the death of his wife. No other visitor was known to have stayed there. Since he'd lost his wife, he had lived quite alone, spending evenings in the hotel, spinning his yarns: a local character.

And his wife . . . had she guessed his secrets? A framed photograph of her stood on his dressing-table – a heavy-bodied person with chubby features, accusing eyes, dictatorial chin. One could imagine her treating him like an aberrant child and Caudry playing up to it. In one of two wardrobes her clothes were hanging just as they'd been left, and more clothes of hers were in the drawers, even shoes under the bed. It was her presence, rather than his, that one still sensed in the flat.

Downstairs, the shop was anonymous: you could scarcely have guessed at the man who ran it. Well-stocked, well-displayed, and on the evidence of a day-book, flourishing. But, anonymous. In a corner was a safe that Ringmer was surveying with a frown, but ten to one it contained only material relating to the business. In the counter-drawers, catalogues, receipts; in the till a voucher for the sale I'd seen him pull off that morning – any cash he would surely have pocketed before he made his break. At the same time, cash might become a problem for a man on the run . . .

'I see he banked with Barclays.'

'Yes sir. I'll have a word with them Monday.'

'Sooner is better. He might be tempted to use his cash-point card.'

'Yes sir, that's a point . . .'

But it was Malling who produced a small breakthrough.

'Look sir, this bunch of old letters. I reckon they're from the sister-in law to his wife, and there's a printed address and telephone number.'

So there was: an address in Reading. Ringmer promptly rang the number, listened with slightly gapped mouth to a diatribe coming down the line. He replaced the instrument delicately.

'Don't think he's going to turn up in Reading, sir.'

'He doesn't have friends there.'

'No sir. Lady thinks we should have done him long ago. According to her, when he married her sister he was only after the business, and when her sister died of a stroke it should have been looked into more than it was.'

No friends in Reading. No friends at all. The few letters to Caudry related to the business. For forty years he had lived there his shadowy life, locked up in himself, a man alone. And with him had dwelt the fear that, on Wednesday, had taken shape, had become a reality about to erupt. Could he truly have been said to have lived at all?

'I reckon that's all we can do now, sir. I'll get a sample of his dabs tomorrow.'

'Better leave a man here. Just in case.'

Ringmer hesitated. 'You don't think he'll be back, sir?'

Perhaps. With a man like Caudry, impossible to forecast his reactions. It was not incredible that he might come slinking back, like a dog to its kennel. The exits were barred, the hunt was up, and this his refuge of forty years,

97

while even the police were a better prospect than what his imagination might be prefiguring.

'Leave a man.'

Ringmer detailed one. Then the lights began to go out; in the flat, in the shop and store-room, finally in the empty garage. Malling jiggled the lock of the doors again, to leave them the way we'd found them. Once more, all was dark; and the gapers in the street began to move away.

I bid them goodnight, and dodged traffic across the street to the hotel. Gabrielle was waiting in reception; she was on the watch, and jumped up immediately I appeared.

'And – that is that?'

I shook my head. 'Caudry had hooked it before we got there.'

'He had hooked it?'

'Yes.'

'Then, my dear, it is not one moment too soon.'

She took my arm and steered me to the double glass-doors of the dining room. For an instant, all I was seeing was the crowded room, the busy waiters. Then I spotted them, at a corner table: Madame Bernay and her brother. And, along with them, the four men I'd last seen in a blue Citroen BX.

'And so it is not to London they go, these men who wish for the road to Leyhurst.'

I drew her away from the doors. 'Let's go for a drink!'

'Aha. But that changes nothing.'

She followed me to the bar, however, and graciously accepted a dry sherry. I bought the pint I felt I'd earned, and we took a bench remote from the company.

'Tell me what happened.'

'So. I go to our room to freshen-up, yes? And then, because I do not wish to have my eyes on that shop, I retire to the small lounge that faces the garden. In reception I have bought a newspaper, and in this I am reading about the damage of the storm, when, of a sudden, I am hearing French voices, of which one I am recognising as Madame Bernay's. Ha. I reconnoitre, taking care that I am not seen, and there, in reception, kissing madame with fervour, are these four gentlemen who seek the road to Leyhurst. They are strangers, ha? *Mon pied*! I hear enough. They have arranged to meet here. In the presence of the clerk they do not speak their business, merely condolences to madame, and then he is finding them keys, and, with their baggage, they are departing upstairs.'

'They are booked in, then?'

'But yes. Booked in. All this is no accident, my friend. Madame comes here, and so do they. And you tell me it is not by arrangement?'

'Go on.'

'They are upstairs a long while, and Madame and her brother up there with them. Then they come down to this bar for drinks, but, alas, sit not where I may hear them. Also, though they talk much, it is in low voices, and most solemn are their faces. I stay discreetly out of their vision. At last, they retire to have their meal.'

I quaffed beer. 'It could still be innocent.'

'Oh, oh! They are not strangers to madame.'

'They might have decided to leave London till tomorrow, ran into madame here and heard her story.'

'That is not what I am seeing, not what I am hearing. I repeat, they meet here by arrangement.'

'They could yet be friends, come over to support her.'

'Your Gabrielle says no. And you had best believe her.'

Yes; I better had. Coincidences happen, but here were too many. Four men of the age of men who could have taken part in the wartime resistance: who had followed madame on the next boat: who had shown they knew where to find her. If comedy was what madame had in mind, then now madame was mob-handed. Yet, in Leyhurst, Sussex . . .?

'Did you notice them pay any attention to the shop?'

Reluctantly, Gabrielle hoisted her shoulders. 'But how much longer can it be, my friend? Someone will tell them of a shopkeeping Frenchman.'

'They appear to speak no English.'

'It will not stop them. And doubtless in the town are those who speak French. It is as well that you warn the good Ringmer that the comrades are on his doorstep.'

I drank up. 'Let's see that register!'

We went back into reception. Four names in handwriting that varied from the blottesque to sweeping copper-plate. Messieurs Dreux, Nogent, Houdan and Brezolles. And from Evreux, every one.

'How long have they booked for?'

'Till Monday,' the clerk said. 'But they may be staying on.'

'We'll take the table in the alcove.'

The dining room was still populous when we entered it, but by luck a table was vacant at the end opposite from Madame Bernay's. I wanted to observe, not be observed, and the alcove-table was ideal: close to the door and a little concealed by one of a pair of palms. For Madame Bernay, they'd placed tables together. She sat facing her brother with the newcomers on either hand. Just then they were being helped by waitresses and their attention was on their plates. We gave our order. The wine-waiter came. Gabrielle made her selection. The room was a-buzz with conversation, clink of plates, occasional laughter.

'The man with dyed hair is, I think, their leader.'

He looked like a professional man of some sort; dressed in a well-cut pin-stripe suit, waistcoat, grey bow-tie. He had a plump, jowled face shaded with bristle and alert brown eyes under heavy brows, chattered in a hard voice, flourished knife and fork as he ate.

'What about the big fellow?'

'A farmer.'

100

Sunken cheeks and short, wiry hair. He ate silently, steadily, packing food into a capacious mouth.

'And the fresh-faced one?'

'*Un charcutier*. And I am not meaning a surgeon.'

'And his neighbour?'

'Aha, little mouse-face. He is someone's clerk, perhaps a book-keeper.'

'Well . . . they don't look very dangerous.'

'They are comrades, my friend, not gangsters. Should the moment arrive, you will see. For did they not fool *les Chleuhs*, and live?'

But that had been four decades ago. Tonight, they more resembled a diners' club, with only the circumstance of their chattering in French drawing occasional glances from the neighbouring tables. A few friends, perhaps old school-fellows, with the wife or sister of one of them along: that was how they appeared as the meal progressed, as the wine generously flowed. Most loquacious was the dyed-haired man, who was seated at Madame Bernay's elbow. Sometimes Gabrielle's pork-butcher would put in a word, but the brother and the other two had little to say.

Our food came. At the other table they had got to coffee and liqueurs: Gabrielle nudged me.

'I think the doctor is about to propose a toast.'

'Is he a doctor?'

'It is my guess. See, every glass is being filled.'

And it was impressive. Very slowly, each member of the party rose to their feet, including madame, and, in complete silence, six glasses were raised. For several long moments the tableau was held, and the tables round about also fell silent. Then the dyed-haired man fired off a word which I couldn't catch, but which Gabrielle did, exclaiming:

'*Les morts*! They toast the dead.'

When six glasses swept to six mouths.

'Ah – she sees us!'

With the glass yet at her mouth, Madame Bernay was staring across at our table. Her black eyes flashed, but she said nothing until the six of them were seated again. Then she touched the dyed-haired man's arm, muttered to him, and nodded towards us. His glance was quick but comprehensive, dwelling longest on Gabrielle.

'She has told him that you are a policeman, and he is remembering our encounter this afternoon.'

Indeed, at that table heads were drawn together and there was low and urgent conversation.

'Eat your food.'

'A gesture, my friend.'

'This is not a time for gestures.'

'Ah, but yes!'

And seizing her glass, she rose and raised it towards Madame Bernay. Every eye at that table turned to her, not to mention those from every other: and, after a pause, Madame Bernay rose also, lifted her glass; and together they drank.

'There – that is fitting!'

Face flushed, Gabrielle resumed her seat.

'It was scarcely discreet.'

'You are English, Monsieur George. You do not understand these matters.'

'Here comes something else to be understood.'

The dyed-haired man had got to his feet. Looking straight ahead, he crossed the room, halted at our table and clicked his heels.

'Madame. Monsieur.'

'Monsieur.'

'I have the pleasure to introduce myself. My name is Bertrand Brezolles and I am a notary from Evreux. Madame had the kindness to assist myself and my friends this afternoon, and it appears that monsieur and madame are acquainted also with our townswoman, Madame Bernay, and her brother. Thus it is my additional pleasure to invite monsieur and madame, when their meal

102

shall be completed, to join us for a drink in the smaller lounge.'

'Monsieur,' Gabrielle said. 'Convey our compliments to Madame Bernay. On behalf of my husband and myself, we accept your gracious invitation.'

'Madame. Monsieur.'

'Monsieur.'

He made a small bow, and marched back to the other table. All this before forty silent diners, a selection of waiters and a pop-eyed *maître d'hôtel*.

Then the surf of conversation slowly returned, with some amused comments and nervous giggles.

'They mean to put on an act, my friend.'

Well, they seemed to be adepts at that. A few minutes later they rose from their table and, led by Madame Bernay and Brezolles, left the dining room.

Half-an-hour later, we joined them. They had got the little lounge to themselves. They sat disposed around a low coffee-table where stood bottles of liqueurs and a dish of *petit-fours*. The men rose as we entered and Brezolles performed introductions. The fresh-faced man, Lucien Dreux, was indeed a pork-butcher, but Gabrielle's farmer, one Claude Nogent, turned out to be a building contractor. Emile Houdan, the slight, small-featured man, was introduced as a civil servant, retired.

'And you, monsieur,' Brezolles addressed me, 'are, I understand, a man of distinction, an officer of police of high rank, though not, I am told, of the local gendarmerie. You are here with madame on vacation, monsieur?'

'Let us say in the role of observer.'

'Of observer, yes. I understand. To ascertain that the underlings perform their duty.'

He had a cigar going. He poured me a Calvados. Madame Bernay watched all with mean eyes. Clearly this was to be Brezolles' party and she had probably been warned to keep the peace. I accepted a cigar along with the Calvados; Gabrielle had been provided with an anisette and Gauloise.

'Madame is perhaps wondering why we are not in London?'

'Monsieur is correct,' Gabrielle said flatly.

'Madame, that is easily explained. It is, of course, our intention to proceed there later. However, we had heard of the lamentable tragedy that had befallen our renowned fellow-townsman, also that his distraught widow was to be found at this hotel. Thus, we agreed to break our journey here, to offer any assistance and comfort she might need, and, indeed, out of simple respect to the memory of a man admired by us all.'

'That was thoughtful of you, monsieur.'

'Madame, we mourn the death of a great spirit. The more so since it occurred in a manner so bizarre and so fortuitous.'

'By an Act of God.'

He bowed his head. 'To every man must come his fate. In this must be a lesson to us all. In the midst of life, there is death.'

'Oh, what nonsense!' Madame Bernay burst out. 'Pierre was murdered, Bertrand, and you know it.'

Brezolles shrugged, very French. 'Poor madame is distraught, cannot easily accept what has happened to her man.'

'Darlan killed him. The world knows it.'

'Darlan, Darlan. He is dead, madame. Would the Gestapo have left him alive after his purpose had been served?'

'He was here. Pierre discovered him.'

'Just a man who resembled him, no more.'

'Not so, the man himself – as this policeman here very well knows.'

'There, there, madame, there, there!' Brezolles was in haste to wave her down. 'Poor madame, her grief is understandable, explanations she must find for such a

104

tragedy. But, after all? Pierre meets a man who reminds him of a traitor, long since dead. That is all. Then a falling tree kills him, but that is no hand reaching out from the grave. No, madame, no. It serves no purpose to repeat such rumours.'

And Madame Bernay bit her lips together, though her eyes were flashing black fire.

I sipped my Calvados, which was not of the best, and puffed my cigar, which was. Very casually, I said:

'Such a man as Darlan was living in this town.'

Every eye hit mine: Brezolles froze in the act of lifting his glass to his mouth.

'Such a man . . .?'

'A French expatriate who, for many years, kept a shop here.'

'A shop!' Brezolles was recovering. 'Yes – then, perhaps, this will present an explanation! A French expatriate, yes, in a shop poor Pierre could well have met him. But – he is not here now?'

I shook my head.

'But, nevertheless, this explains everything. A shopkeeper who Pierre met, and who bore a passing resemblance to the traitor Darlan. Is not that what he told your brother, madame?'

Madame Bernay spat. 'Where is that man?'

'That man has left town.'

'You lie. He is here.'

'You will not find that man in Leyhurst.'

'Then you are protecting him!'

I shook my head.

'Yes! You are giving that traitor protection. He killed Pierre, and this you know, yet still are giving him protection.'

'Against whom, madame?'

'Whom – ?'

'Madame, madame!' Brezolles interrupted. 'It does no good, these wild ravings, you will make monsieur think

105

you are a mad woman. It is an innocent shopkeeper of whom we are speaking, not of traitors who died in the war.'

'I cannot be silent, Bertrand – '

'Good Madame Simone, you must be patient.'

'Too long I am patient!'

But, with an effort, she buttoned her lips tight again.

'So, so,' Brezolles waffled. 'We have an explanation of these vexed matters, and, perhaps, it is as well that this poor shopkeeper is out of town.'

I sipped; I puffed.

'This man was a comrade.'

Once more Brezolles' glass was frozen.

'He . . . a comrade?'

I nodded. 'But were you not also one, Monsieur Brezolles?'

'Oh, monsieur!'

'Were you not?'

'We do not talk much of such things, these days. It is all long ago, yes? A tale for old men in chimney corners.'

'Yet, in Evreux, isn't there a society of veteran comrades of the Resistance – a society of which, I am informed, the dead man was the president?'

'It is a small thing, a bagatelle –'

'But you are a member?'

His shoulders swayed.

'And you also, messieurs, you are members – perhaps even monsieur, madame's brother?'

Only Madame Bernay's eye was meeting mine.

I sipped.

'So, messieurs, comes this call from your president in England. He has seen a man who greatly resembles the infamous betrayer of Trouville. He is not sure, he will watch this man, but then, mysteriously, he dies. And his colleagues arrive on a shopping trip, broken only to comfort his grieving widow. Is this the picture I am looking at, messieurs?'

106

'Monsieur, I am shocked –'

'Are you armed, monsieur?'

'Monsieur!'

From Madame Bernay an ironic, gravelly chuckle.

I sipped. 'I'm waiting for an answer.'

Brezolles drew himself up haughtily. 'Monsieur, I am insulted as well as shocked, but, in answer to your question, no. We are civilised people, monsieur, who come to your country for a civilised purpose, and who, at the present moment, are engaged in a mission that is purely humane.'

'You are not here by arrangement?'

'Already I have explained.'

'Yet, you are booked in for an indefinite period.'

'That is of small consequence! We remain here, monsieur, while this distressed lady has need of our assistance and our support.' He slammed down his glass. 'Has monsieur no feelings? Is it nothing that madame is in grief and in shock? Is it nothing that we have lost a friend in what monsieur admits are mysterious circumstances? If that is so, monsieur, then be advised, we are also here to see justice done, and, if a crime has indeed been committed, to see the miscreant locked in a cell.'

'And should that miscreant be Darlan?'

He hauled up short. 'Monsieur must know that Darlan is dead.'

'But if he is alive?'

'That cannot be. The Gestapo dealt with him long since.'

'But . . . supposing?'

'Then, then, monsieur –' Brezolles threw back his head in an ecstasy of hauteur – 'then, I shall spit in the face of that man, and hurl after him the reproaches of all France. Is monsieur answered?'

I gazed at him steadily; at the goggling eyes of the contractor; at the frowning stare of the pork-butcher, the squint of the civil servant (retired).

'Messieurs,' I said. 'I see a picture, which may be false, may be true. But such a warning as I gave madame I shall now give to you. Messieurs, you will leave this matter to the English police, and in no way seek to interfere. Failing that, you will certainly be arrested and deported back to France. To each one of you this is clear?'

Brezolles made to jump in, but then he thought better of it.

'Clear?'

The response came in a chorus, with even the brother joining in. Only Madame kept her mouth tight shut.

'Then now we understand each other.' I stubbed out my cigar, beckoned to Gabrielle, and together we left the small lounge.

'But, my dear, you do not believe such an act as that lawyer was putting on?'

We were back in the bar, where, with bitter, I was cleansing from my mouth the taste of that Calvados.

I shook my head. 'It could just be true, cutting a corner here and there. Spitting in Darlan's face could be the limit of their ambitions.'

'Then you heard nothing, saw nothing, my friend. You had best listen to your good French wife. They will spit in Darlan's face, oh yes, but not until he is dangling from a tree.'

'That's true of madame.'

'But yes. And madame, you shall see, will rule the others. For one, the butcher will be her man, and, also, I did not like the big peasant.'

'At the same time . . .'

'Believe me.'

'Perhaps a word with Frénaye is in order.'

'Aha. That is wisdom. He can perhaps tell the history of these people.'

The phones were in reception, not so far from the door of the small lounge; through the glass panels I could partly see the scene we had just left. They had drawn their chairs closer together and were deep in earnest conversation. At their centre, Madame Bernay, whose harsh voice I could just distinguish.

'Alloo . . .?'

'Gently here.'

'Ah, monsieur! You have been much in my thoughts this last day. Also that vile man you spoke of, the traducer of poor Bernay. You have news of this man?'

In a few words I outlined the situation. Frénaye heard me in silence, but gave an exclamation when I named the four men who were sitting in the lounge.

'Ha, monsieur! Then the Musketeers are with you.'

'The Musketeers . . .?'

'But yes. They are called The Four Musketeers of Evreux. All are comrades, who, amongst them, ran the resistance group in the town, and who now form the committee, of which Bernay was chairman, of the Society of the Comrades. And they too are in England?'

'Indeed they are.'

'I trust, Monsieur George, they give you no trouble.'

'Should I be expecting it?'

Frénaye hesitated, and I could picture the cautious look in his soft eyes.

'Monsieur, I do not know quite how to answer that. In these days their organisation is mainly social. The comrades themselves are growing elderly, and unfitted for such exploits as formerly. Yet, old feelings linger on, and rash actions are not unheard of. And, in the case of such an animal as the traducer, an act of avengement may appear heroic.'

'In so many words, do you think they've come for him?'

'Monsieur, in your place, I would have an eye kept on them. And this also remember, their reach stretches far, there are comrades found in many places.'

I paused. 'Like the D.S.T.?'

Frénaye paused too. 'Even there, monsieur. I shall not ask why you enquire.'

'Thank you, Frénaye.'

'Monsieur.'

I hung up, then rang Ringmer, who sounded unimpressed by what I had to tell him.

'Between you and me, sir, if these froggies can find him, it would save us a deal of sweat.'

'No luck so far?'

'Not a dicky. He certainly wasn't on the boat to Dieppe. Portsmouth picked up a frog in a Ford, but he was only a tourist on his way home.'

I hung up again, glanced into the small lounge: still the inmates were locked in fervent discussion. Then, as I was about to rejoin Gabrielle, my eye fell on a customer booking-in at the desk.

A man.

A man whom I knew.

A man whose face I would never forget.

And then he turned, and saw me: Superintendent Cartier. Of the *Direction de la Surveillance du Territoire*.

At once he looked away, grabbed a bag and was heading for the stairs: but I was there before him. We stood at the foot of the stairs, confronting each other.

8

'So, monsieur, I have the grave displeasure of meeting you again. I cross the Channel for a few days of leisure, and, at once, am running into monsieur.'

He hadn't changed. The same staring blue eyes, bland face, air of lurking violence. A thick-necked, heavy-shouldered figure, lips curled in a sneer.

'It won't do, Cartier.'

'Monsieur? But, no doubt, I should be feeling honoured! It is perhaps the memory of our exploits in France that finds you waiting here to greet me.'

'You aren't here on pleasure.'

'A few days, monsieur. And the autumn weather now so clement. But, an encounter with Monsieur Gently is not one of the pleasures I am promising myself.'

Luckily, we were out of sight of the bar, where Gabrielle was waiting for me. Somehow, she would have to be prepared for a possible meeting with this sinister man. My heart beat faster at the thought: she'd seen him last with a smoking gun in his hand: an image with which she had connected me, and which had nearly been her destruction. I said:

'Monsieur, we will go to your room. What we have to discuss is not public property. Should you refuse, I shall have the trouble of arresting you and of escorting you to the police station.'

'Monsieur, you would not dare.'

'Monsieur, you had best not try me.'

The blue eyes were deadly for a moment, then he shrugged. And we went up the stairs.

Among its other conveniences The Swinburne had miniature bars in the bedrooms, and Cartier, after throwing down his bag, went to pour himself a cognac. He didn't offer me one. He went to stare through the window before drawing the curtains with care. I had closed the door behind us. He came back into the room. He said:

'Let me tell you something, monsieur. On that day you will remember in the forest of St. Gatien, your fate should have been the same as Starnberg's. So nearly it was. It needed no sentimentalist to survive to tell tales. An exchange of fire, a dead terrorist, and, how unfortunate, a dead *Anglais*.'

I said nothing.

'But you survived,' Cartier said. 'And because of this my career was in jeopardy. I, who trapped the terrorist Starnberg, was suspended, reprimanded and denied promotion.'

I said: 'There was another witness.'

'Indeed yes. A hysterical woman.'

'Another stray bullet?'

'The woman was suspect and her testimony would not have been believed.'

'She is now my wife.'

The blue stare was contemptuous. 'So! A sentimentalist to the end. And doubtless she looks upon you as a hero, and the extinction of terrorists as a crime. But no matter. Of these things I remind you to show that I owe you few favours. But they are old tales, I am prepared to forget them, I wish them not to sour a pleasant vacation.' He stuck out a hand. 'Shall it not be so?'

I looked at the hand. 'No thank you.'

'Monsieur, I could resent that. But I shall not. It is not my business here to seek trouble.'

'Then what is your business?'

112

'It is as I said. A few days of leisure in your country.'

'But after the lies?'

He glared: shrugged; went to the bar to freshen his glass. He had on a floppy, Italian-style jacket which might well be concealing an armpit holster: I couldn't decide. But when he turned from the bar he was wearing a more conciliatory expression.

'Monsieur, we are two professionals, let us cease to play foolish games! I find you here at this hotel, almost as though it is by appointment. Also, in the register, I see the name of the widow of a Frenchman recently dead, along with that of her brother, and those of four gentlemen from Evreux. This is no coincidence. It stinks of the comrades, of whom the dead man was one. Let us clear the air, monsieur. I believe our interests are not incompatible.'

'Go on,' I said.

'It comes to our knowledge that in this town lives a French expatriate, one using the name of Jean Caudry, who departed from France after the war.'

'The knowledge came to you how?'

'Let me proceed! By chance the dead man, Bernay, met this Caudry, and, it seems, identified him as a collaborator, Gustave Darlan. Clearly, Darlan had to silence this man, and did so, it appears with ingenuity. It may even be, monsieur, that the death is still regarded by you as accidental.'

'And you know it is not?'

'In good time! Unluckily, Bernay had informed the comrades, thus Darlan, who, in the Occupation, had given material assistance to the Germans, was in danger of assassination, and so has been obliged to depart from this town.'

'Which, also, you know?'

'Monsieur, I shall explain. But first, we compare our information. Do I understand that Bernay's death has been investigated, and that now you are seeking Darlan to answer for it?'

Reluctantly, I nodded.

'You have a solid case?'

'A case that will lead to conviction. But, monsieur, I have yet to learn how you come to be so very well informed.'

'Yes, yes.'

He juggled with the bottle again, but this time to fill a glass for me. Then he pointed to the only chair, and himself took a seat on the bed. He raised his glass.

'To our good understanding!'

I raised my glass, but didn't drink. Cartier chose not to notice, sipped, sat warming the glass between his palms. After a moment his stare fixed mine.

'Consider, if you please, this man's position! His cover, so long successful, is blown, and he has the comrades but one step behind him. In addition he is wanted by the English police, who have an unanswerable case against him. His situation is desperate, but he holds one card, he knows the identity of some former collaborators – men, it may be, now holding high office, and with credentials apparently impeccable. A good card! But how shall he play it? The comrades would love dearly to have those names. Then would follow a series of outrages, bombs, snipings, to be diplomatically blamed on Arab terrorists. But would that buy off Darlan? My dear colleague, no. They would settle with Darlan just the same. So, if he wishes to survive, he must play a different hand.'

I gazed at him. 'You?'

Cartier drank.

I said: 'Are you telling me you've spoken with Darlan?'

His shoulders twitched. 'At two pm today a telephone was ringing in my office. Do not ask me from where he rings, it is a call-box, that is all. But soon I am listening to a deal which I cannot easily refuse.'

'What deal?'

'Oh, monsieur!'

'He is expecting you to lift him out?'

114

'What else? And furthermore, to arrange for him a renewed cover. It is not impossible. A pleasant retirement in one of our sunnier dependencies, there to bask with a remittance, far away from the knowledge of the comrades.'

'And – you agreed?'

'But, dear colleague, of course.'

'To get those names, you would do what he wants?'

'Please, do not be naive. I am content he shall rest in an English gaol. But to stop his mouth is vital. One name he gave me by way of sample. It is that of a minister who, at this moment, is engaged in delicate and critical negotiations. It is my duty, monsieur, to protect that man in both his life and his reputation, and the two will assuredly be at risk if Darlan is allowed to point a finger.'

'Which he threatened to do?'

'Naturally. That was the deal I could not refuse. Either I agreed to his demands, or he would seek the hospitality of the English press. What would follow I need scarcely say. It might well lead to the downfall of the administration, with the certainty of outrages and the possibilities of civil unrest.'

'But the names you require as well as his silence.'

'Such information is our business.'

'Information of great utility.'

Cartier merely shrugged. 'Thus, I confer with my masters, and we do not let the grass grow. A charter plane takes me to Lydd, where a rented car is waiting. Meanwhile the *Département* is in contact with the local police chief – oh yes, my presence is official – and here I shall await a favourable development, with, I trust, police cooperation.'

I said: 'When and where do you meet him?'

'Monsieur, that problem is out of my hands. He describes to me his shop across the street, but now, of course, that is out of the question.'

'It was so when he rang you.'

115

'I do not know. I shall, naturally, cooperate with the police. With them the *Département* will make arrangements for me to question him upon his arrest.'

'And until then?'

'I wait.'

I shook my head. 'Monsieur is taking me for a fool.'

The blue eyes rested on mine uncharitably. But all Cartier did was sip his drink.

I said: 'Darlan was also a professional, and he is not a man to rely on chance. If he was expecting you to spring him then he would have arranged a time and place. Furthermore, you can't wait until we arrest him, because if you fail him he'll ring the press. And the odds are, if we arrest him first, that he will never open his mouth to you.'

Cartier nodded his head very slowly. 'Then Monsieur is not entirely a man of sentiment! But with regard to the last point, the odds are good that Darlan will open his mouth to me. I still bring him promise of succour, monsieur, even when he is sitting in a cell – the *Département* is prepared to fund his defence, and, should he be released, provide the cover he requires. But, as to the rest, there is of course much in what monsieur says.'

'So?'

'So. I will lay out my cards. Darlan did not specify a place. He instructed me to stay in this hotel, and here to await from him a message.'

'What form of message?'

'He didn't say. A call on the telephone is the most likely. And then, I must be ready with a car to drive him at once to the place he shall tell me.'

'Of which, of course, he gave no indication.'

'It is, we may suppose, not too many miles.'

'And, if this had worked out?'

'Monsieur?'

'If this clandestine meeting had taken place?'

The blue eyes didn't flicker.

'Then, monsieur, I would have obtained the information I require. After which I would have arrested Darlan and turned him over to you, with my compliments.'

'Even though he might talk to us – and subsequently, to our intelligence?'

The eyes exploded. 'Monsieur – I am trusting you!'

I stared him down. 'Come off it, Cartier. Once you'd got what you wanted from Darlan, his life wouldn't be worth a row of beans. You'd want him silenced, and the comrades are here to do the job or take the blame. Then you'd have been down the road to Lydd and on your plane back to Paris.'

He jumped off the bed: swung away from me. 'Monsieur,' he said softly, 'you are learning lessons. Perhaps, back there in the forest, the bullet would have found the wrong man. Yes, I would wish Darlan dead. That is the logic of the matter. Nor do I very much care if the comrades claim their own. But the case has altered, monsieur. By an evil turn, I run into you. I am left now with no alternative but to wait my chance when the man is arrested. I do not say I would have played it different, but I cannot play it different now. So, I am here to cooperate. And to seek cooperation from you.'

'How much cooperation?'

He sat down again. 'This man must be kept from your intelligence. In their hands, his information would be a mine-field waiting to be exploded. They might not use it, but it would remain there, a threat they would know we dare not ignore. In all future negotiations our administration would be looking over its shoulder.'

I nodded. 'And, in your hands?'

'That is a different matter, monsieur! In our hands it will be used constructively, for the proper purposes of the state.'

I bowed my head.

'Then, this is agreed?'

'It can be agreed so far, monsieur. That, should our intelligence wish to question Darlan, it will be under the eye of this police authority.'

'They cannot remove him?'

'No.'

'Then that is sufficient, monsieur. After I have talked to him he will keep his mouth shut, in order to retain our support. That I may interrogate him is likewise agreed?'

'Also in the presence of this authority.'

He hesitated. 'Monsieur, in that way information may be leaked. I may not question him alone?'

'With one senior officer.'

'Then, I must insist it shall be you, who, as a sentimentalist, I think I may trust.'

I bowed again. 'And for your part, monsieur?'

'Monsieur, I become your contact-man. To me, and to me only, Darlan is prepared to reveal his hiding-place. In this hotel I shall await his message according to our agreement, and, when I receive it, pass the intelligence to you. Is this not sufficient?'

'Two other things, monsieur. You are aware of certain fellow guests in this hotel. You will undertake to hold no communication with the widow Bernay and the men from Evreux. That is the first thing.'

'Monsieur is joking. Their affairs have no utility for me. And the second thing?'

'You will maintain the greatest possible distance from my wife.'

His stare was long and incredulous. 'You do not take me for a rival, monsieur?'

'Just give me your undertaking.'

'Then, as you wish. I shall cast no eyes at madame your wife. But you continue to surprise me, monsieur. Your sentimentality indeed runs deep. However, such conditions I freely accept, and now, I take it, we are agreed.'

'We are agreed.'

'In which case, monsieur, you will permit me to bid you adieu. Doubtless you will have arrangements to make, while I am detained from a much-delayed meal.'

I bowed. 'Monsieur.'

He bowed. 'Monsieur.'

I quitted the room and left him to it.

And I was trusting him about as far as I could throw him.

I went down directly to the phones. Ringmer was out, but from the duty man I got the Chief Constable's private number. Some delay! Fretting, I noticed that the small lounge now was empty, and, while I hung on, Gabrielle came to the door of the bar. I made a smile and waved her back again – soon, probably, Cartier would be passing through reception – and she made a little face towards the phone before retreating into the bar again.

'Hullo – Gently? What's all this? I've got a dinner-party on here, man.'

'I'm sorry, sir, but this is urgent. We need a tap on the Swinburne Hotel.'

'A what?'

'A tap on the phones, sir, at the earliest possible moment.'

'But, look here! What's it about? We can't just go round tapping people's phones . . .'

As briefly as I could I put the position, and mention of the D.S.T. got him going: the call was transferred to his study, the sounds of background festivities cut.

'This fellow Cartier – is he the frog they've sent over?'

'He's here with a brief to meet Caudry. Caudry rang Paris to set up a deal. He gives them names, they lift him out.'

'But – hang it! – I can't take this in. Are you sure that someone isn't pulling our leg?'

'I've spoken to Cartier, who promises cooperation. Caudry will contact him at The Swinburne.'

'Then why are we tapping it?'

'Because we can't trust Cartier.'

119

'But surely the fellow will play along?'

'Once Cartier has got his information, Caudry's career may not be very prolonged. His silence would best suit Cartier, and four more French comrades have shown up at the hotel.'

'But this is getting damned ridiculous, Gently. You mean he'd unload these other frogs on him?'

'Yes sir.'

'We have to take this seriously?'

'Yes sir. And we urgently need that tap.'

I convinced him at last. About Cartier's compliance there was too much that gave grounds for caution. The more one thought about it, the plainer it became that Caudry/Darlan's card had already been marked. Meeting me, Cartier had had to adjust his game, but it was a game he still meant to play. Even his account of the deal with Caudry had a fishy smell in my nostrils. I went out to the yard. Only one car there, a brown Montego, bore rental plates: I memorised the number, went back to the phone, and this time succeeded in raising Ringmer. I gave him the picture.

'We shall need a tail car.'

'I'll do my best, sir. But we're stretched at the moment.'

'Cartier can take us straight to Caudry.'

'I appreciate that, sir. But won't we be getting the message on the phone-tap?'

'There may not be a message. Cartier is no fool, he'll know our first move will be bugging the phone. Either he has a rendezvous already set up, or an alternative method for contracting Caudry. If there's a message, it could be a blind. What we really need is a bug on the car.'

'Don't know if I can raise one of those, sir.'

I knew who could: but it wasn't an option. 'So, a tail car.'

'As soon as I can, sir. And I'll brief the patrols to watch out.'

It wasn't good enough but it would have to do: and meanwhile my own eye would be on Cartier. Once more I left the phone-booth to rejoin Gabrielle in the bar. And I was too late. She was back in reception, staring through the panels in the dining room doors: at a dining room unlit except in one corner, where sat a heavy, bull-necked figure.

'My friend, I am seeing a ghost.'

I'd tried to put my arm round her, but Gabrielle had thrust me away. She was trembling slightly, cheeks paled, her hazel eyes rounded. Cartier hadn't seen us. He had his back to the doors, was hungrily wolfing a plate of salad. The only other person present was a waitress, who sat across the room, boredly eyeing a magazine.

'I had hoped to warn you – come away!'

She shook her head, and went on staring. Her breathing was quick, her hands balled; she seemed almost intolerant of my presence. And, of course, I knew what she was seeing as she stared at that man crouched over his plate. I was seeing it too, the scene in the forest, the bloodied body at Cartier's feet.

'Why – why is he here?'

'Caudry did a deal with him.'

'Then, the fool is as good as dead.'

'Through him, we hope to reach Caudry.'

'His body only will you find.'

'Come away.'

'No, my friend. I face this terrible man at last. Till this moment I live with him behind me, that shall be no more. We are face to face.'

'What would you do?'

'I must meet him.'

'Gabrielle! He has promised to stay away from you.'

'But no, he shall not. I will not fear him. Now, he must also meet me.'

I caught at her arm, but she threw me off and made a sudden dive through the doors. And at once she was across the room and standing, arms akimbo, before Cartier. Cartier jerked back in his chair. The bland face was an empty mask. Then slowly he laid down knife and fork, glanced at me, rose to his feet.

'Madame. Monsieur. You are impatient to see me?'

'Look upon me, monsieur,' Gabrielle said.

'I see you, madame –'

'Then, monsieur, you are looking at a woman who despises a loathsome animal. In this town lived the traitor Darlan, a creature so low that I would not spit on him. But higher he stands in the human scale than one I see before me now.'

'Madame, beware –'

'Ha, beware! You will deal with me as you have with some others? For shame, monsieur, if shame you can feel. As I feel shame that you are a Frenchman. What you are I have seen, and what I am you see now. And this you shall receive from an honest woman who once was betrayed in your murderous plots.'

And, before either of us could stop her, she had slapped his face twice. Immediately, he sprang towards her, and, as quickly, my arm was encircling his throat. The waitress, forgotten, gave a low scream; but the business was over in a moment. Cartier broke free, stood panting, massaging the angry glow in his cheeks.

'If this were in France – !'

'But it is not, monsieur.' Gabrielle made the motion of wiping her hands. 'And now I feel cleaner, sweeter, and purged of such men as are called Cartier. Remember me, monsieur. For I shall no more remember you.'

Then she turned, and walked leisurely across the room and through the doors. Cartier's eyes were savage.

'Monsieur, for this I blame you! Had I not given you my word that I would avoid contact with that woman?'

122

I shrugged. 'She had other ideas. For which I continue to admire her.'

'Then, monsieur, you must watch your back, for this insult shall not go unrewarded.'

I shook my head. 'You'll toe the line, Cartier. Because you need that cooperation. Just remember that the line to M.I.5 starts at the telephone-booth out there!'

'Also, monsieur, you need *my* cooperation!'

'Only, I think you need mine most. So you'd best get quietly back to your meal and forget what has just happened here.'

For an instant the blue eyes looked dangerous: then he ghosted a shrug.

'Perhaps, as you say, it is best. Men are fools who lose their temper over a woman. Our affairs are more important, monsieur, and we must not allow ourselves to be diverted. No doubt you have this matter well in hand?'

'Of that monsieur may be certain.'

'So, I will finish my interrupted meal, and trust the waitress will not be alarmed again.'

I followed Gabrielle. She was waiting on the stairs, and preceded me to our room. But, once we were inside, she fell weeping into my arms.

'Forgive me, my dear. For once I am weak. But of sudden, my whole world seems to have changed.'

The light was too garish and I switched it off: we sat in the dim glow reflected from the street.

'Since the great wind, nothing is the same. Our small home in London is a foreign place. My new country, it seems, has been raped, and from my old country come only monsters. At moments I do not know who I am, except in part the wife of this man here.'

'We will leave.'

'Not even that can I do. In some small way, I am feeling responsible. For am I not a compatriot of these people, and

123

the daughter of a man of the Resistance? But yes, but yes. They are my people. The old traitor who the storm seemed to expose. The widow and the men who hunt him. Even the man of death below.'

'Their being French doesn't make you responsible.'

'I know only that I cannot leave. As though I am the appointed conscience of all, and must stay by until the end. But will you not laugh at foolish Gabrielle?'

'Why would I laugh?'

'Because a fool I am. Your brave girl is no more a brave girl, and wishes only the comfort of your arms.'

That at least she had. She wept a little longer. I found a handkerchief to dry her eyes. Over her head I was looking through our window to the shadowy building across the street.

'That man.'

'Forget that man.'

'You do not mean to let him get to the shopkeeper?'

'We have taken precautions. A tail on his car. A monitor on the telephone. If Caudry contacts him, we shall know. If he has made a rendezvous, we shall follow him.'

'Of this, I am thinking he is well aware.'

'The patrols are also alerted to watch for him. And of course for Caudry. Who may well be picked up before the man downstairs can make a move.'

'Perhaps it is best to let him find the shopkeeper, for the one to be the fate of the other.'

I shook my head.

'But yes, my dear. Better than that the comrades should find him. They are people more decent, more clean, but compelled by the past to adventure this thing. But the man downstairs is as vile as the other. And would better grace your English gaol.'

'Not a point of view we can endorse!'

'So hold me tight. And make me forget him.'

'As for the comrades, they have no lead, and Frénaye is inclined to think they may be harmless.'

124

But we hadn't quite done with Cartier. Almost an hour later, while Gabrielle, thankfully, was cleaning her teeth, came a tap on our door, and I opened it to see his leering face.

'I trust the moment is not inopportune, monsieur.'

He was clad in pyjamas and the sloppy jacket. Now the bland cheeks were less grey and he was exuding an odour of after-shave.

'If you want something, make it quick.'

'I come, monsieur, but to reassure your mind. No doubt your arrangements are entirely adequate, but I would not wish you to lose sleep.'

'So?'

'After a day so interesting, a little assistance in dropping off? Here I have veronal tablets, my usual recourse in these circumstances. You shall see me take them – one, two, and rest assured I will be here in the morning.'

And he unscrewed a tube he was carrying, and popped two tablets into his mouth.

'*Bonne nuit, monsieur.*'

He leered, and went. The tube had certainly been labelled 'veronal'. But the tablets . . .?

I closed the door softly.

If they'd been sweets, I hoped they might poison him.

9

'My dear, I have rung Mrs. Jarvis, and the roads to our house are freshly cleared. Also, though the power is still off, we have not entirely lost our beech tree.'

Indeed, the Sunday after the great storm was almost insulting in its gentleness; untrammelled sun lit the town, the Downs, and the faint sou'wester was soft as Spring.

Much earlier I'd rung the police station to learn if the night had produced any incident. Just one on record: a phone call made by someone to Caudry's flat.

'About two this morning, sir.' It was Malling who'd answered me. 'Our man took it, but the chummie rang off. It was a call made from a phone-box.'

'Local?'

'Couldn't say, sir. Chiefy reckons it could have been Moossoo checking. And like that he probably wasn't too far away, but there's been no report of any sighting.'

'You still have a tail on Cartier's car?'

'Oh yes, sir. Been on all night.'

Veronal or peppermint drops, Cartier was certainly still there in the morning; at breakfast, he it was who had taken the alcove table and was observing, blank-faced, the contingent from Evreux. Had there been contact? The Musketeers, for their part, seemed not to notice his existence. This morning they appeared more subdued, though we caught speaking looks from Madame Bernay. Cartier, having finished his breakfast, strolled through to reception and bought a newspaper. With this, and a

126

cigar, he settled down on a bench by the desk. And the telephone.

'Some game that man is playing, my friend.'

Yes: it was all too relaxed, too casual. Yet we had him covered, the phone, the car: what loophole remained for him to exploit?

'Stay here. I'll have a word with him.'

I went to seat myself beside him. For a while he went on scanning his paper. Then he reached out to tap ash from his cigar.

'You wish to hold my hand, monsieur?'

I said: 'With monsieur, can one be too careful?'

He shrugged, tapped some more ash, hoisted his paper up a notch. I said:

'At breakfast, your eyes took a certain direction.'

'Let us say the amateurs amuse me, monsieur.'

'They could also be useful.'

'To me, no, monsieur. For do you not have me in a cleft stick? I am a tethered goat, I can make no move, I am reduced to a police contact. So I am bored, I watch the amateurs, and am hoping it may not be for too long.'

'A tethered goat may need footloose friends.'

'Doubtless monsieur is expert in such matters.'

'Also, as between information and silence, I am wondering if monsieur may not prefer the latter.'

He tweaked the newspaper impatiently. 'Monsieur, this is a foolish conversation! You have taken these matters out of my hands, cannot you now be content? I wait, I do your bidding, and you may watch me if you will, but, I find your company vexatious. And you interrupt my appraisal of the news.'

At which point the telephone rang: but it was to me that the desk-clerk signalled. I picked it up to find an excited-sounding Ringmer on the other end.

'Sir, Moossoo has been in touch! He rang the shop a few minutes ago, only he wouldn't talk to us.'

'No doubt who it was?'

127

'No sir. He asked if you were still in town. He said he'd only talk to you, and then he hung up pretty smartly.'

I glanced back at Cartier's hunched figure, the straight line of his cigar-smoke.

'I'll be over.'

'If you would, sir. This could be the break we're after.'

I hung up. Cartier ignored me. I rejoined Gabrielle. I said:

'Caudry has rung in, asking for me. I'll be over at the police station.'

Her eyes were large. 'Then I shall watch this man.'

'If he makes a move, ring me.'

Then, always a sentimentalist, I kissed her before going.

I left by way of the car park, where, along with the Montego, sat the two cars from Evreux, the blue Citroen and the white Renault. Across the street sat an unmarked Escort, with a driver who stared at me over his newspaper: the stopper in the bottle. I merely gave him an eyes-left as I went by. Everything in order: so why was I uneasy, going over it again and again in my mind? Just that I knew Cartier was the best, and that I would need to be better to hold him in check. I had seen him operate; this was the man who had outmanoeuvred a top terrorist. Then shot him in cold blood: perhaps it was the ruthlessness I couldn't fathom.

I found Ringmer in his office along with Malling and a bright-eyed detective-constable.

'D.C. Firle, sir . . . it was him who took the call at the flat.'

'A call from a phone-box?'

'Yes sir,' Firle said. 'And it didn't sound very far away.'

'So shoot.'

'At first it was just breathing, sir, then he said "Is that a policeman?" I said "Who's speaking, sir?" – but I'd recognised his voice right away. Then he said "The policeman from London, is he still in Leyhurst?" I said I thought you were, sir, and then he said he wanted to speak to you. I told him I could take a message, but he wasn't having that, so

128

then I asked him how you could contact him, and he rang off at once.'

'And you were quite positive who it was?'

'Yes, sir. I've known Moossoo since I was a nipper.'

'No mention of him ringing back?'

'No sir. Just what I've told you.'

'I'd say he'd got the seconds,' Ringmer said. 'There's too much piling up against him. Now he's yearning for a nice comfy cell where his froggy mates can't get at him.'

'In that case, why ask for me?'

'Because you're the one he's talked to, sir. The one who knows about froggy business. But I reckon in the end he'll make do with us.'

I shook my head. 'Caudry isn't that simple. If he wants me, then it's probably a deal.'

'A deal, sir?'

'An alternative deal. In case the one with Cartier doesn't come off.'

'Not sure I'm with you, sir,' Ringmer said.

I said: 'Just remember that Caudry is no innocent. He's a man who has mixed with the Gestapo and knows what makes such people tick. So he's done a deal with the D.S.T. which could credibly get him out of the country, but now he'll be wondering what's going to happen to him when he's parted with his information. It could be a hint dropped to the comrades. And even that might be a refinement.'

All three were staring at me. Ringmer said:

'But could something like that really happen, sir?'

'It could happen. And sitting in The Swinburne is a man who has made such things happen.'

'But . . . if Caudry suspects?'

'His situation is desperate. He will try to make the deal water-tight of course. But the odds are he can't, and if he can't then he'll need a fall-back deal.'

'But . . . what sort of deal?'

'I can think of two options. Our intelligence could also use his information. But with the comrades waiting on the sidelines he'd think the same objection might apply. So he will most likely go for the second, what in the States they call a plea-bargain. He confesses to killing Bernay, we promote a plea of self-defence.'

'But we couldn't do that, sir!'

'Not on the record. Just pulling the punches would probably do.'

'And – that's what he's after?'

'That's my guess. And he thinks I may have the clout to swing it.'

Ringmer shook his head unhappily. 'Well I don't know, sir! I don't think the C.C. would go along with it. If chummie does ring back we'll have to tell him, he just gives himself up and takes his chances.'

'If Cartier fails him, he may accept that.'

'So then we just have to let him stew, sir. And meanwhile we're pretty certain of one thing, he's still somewhere around the district. Your frog is waiting by the phone, sir?'

'When I left him.'

'Then I reckon we just sit pat. Chummie's nerves are going to beat him, and any time now that phone may ring.'

The phone did ring. Ringmer collared it eagerly, then shrugged and handed it to me. I listened a moment, then said:

'Now we don't sit pat. Cartier's away.'

'Get his tail on the R.T., someone!'

Malling went belting out of the office. On the phone, an indignant Gabrielle was explaining just how she'd been tricked.

'You have gone but minutes, my friend, when he puts down his paper and his cigar. At once I am on the alert, but he pays no attention to me. He stretches himself in a lazy way, then he strolls towards the back lobby, and I, I am keeping him in view, and see him go into the toilet. So I am sitting, I am watching that door, beside the paper, beside the cigar, and moments pass and the cigar is extinguished, but still he does not reappear. Then, suddenly, fool that I am, it is striking me what is going on, and I jump up and run into the toilets, pushing open even the door of the gentlemen's. Nothing. Nobody! And then I see it, a door that opens into the yard. Oh, my friend, I am desolated, but all this time he is getting away.'

'His car has gone?'

'But no. The brown car is in its place. Only, as I rush out into the yard, I am seeing another car driving away, and, though I cannot be assured, I am thinking that man is at the wheel.'

I swore. 'Can you describe it?'

'Alas, my friend, I have not the number. But it is a small hatchback car of a colour between brown and yellow.'

'Which way did it turn?'

'Towards the High Street. But then it is lost from my view.'

'Thank you, you've done well.'

'Oh, my dear, you are married to a fool.'

I hung up. Malling rushed back.

'The frog must still be around. The only car Neville has seen leave in the last fifteen minutes was a dun-coloured Metro.'

'That was Cartier,' I said.

'But it can't have been!'

'It can. He's worked the two-car trick. When he got here yesterday, he parked the rental-car and then went off and hired a Metro. How many garages here rent cars?'

'Just the one,' Malling said. 'And it's Austin-Rover.'

'Try to get the registration. And meanwhile warn the patrols.'

Malling biffed out again. Ringmer was gaping.

'But-look here! The frog would detain Caudry for us, wouldn't he?'

I gave him a stare. 'Apart from anything else, there's a charter-plane standing by at Lydd Airport.'

131

'A charter-plane!'

'Get on to the airport and tell them that plane doesn't leave until we say so. And tell them further to detain any frogs who turn up there in a dun-coloured Metro.'

Ringmer raised the phone and gabbled. But it wasn't only Gabrielle who was kicking herself. It was I who had swallowed that rental-car whole, just as Cartier had intended. There it stood with its beguiling plates for the police to watch till kingdom-come, while, in the same park, waited the humble, anonymous Metro. And for me there was no excuse. I knew, none better, the man we were dealing with. Malling returned.

'I've got the number, sir, and put it out over the air. Chummie was at the garage last thing yesterday, only the name he gave was Lebrun.'

'The name means nothing.'

'He had to show his docs, sir.'

Cartier was a man with plenty of those.

'Did your tail see which way the car turned at the High Street?'

'No sir.'

'Let's look at a map.'

We looked at a map. It told us nothing. That a rendezvous had been arranged in advance was now certain, but unless a proximity to the airport was a factor we might as well make use of a pin. Downs, marshes, lonely beaches: situations for secret encounters abounded. Or by now he could be parked in Brighton. Or trundling into Tunbridge Wells.

'Just keep those patrols on their toes!'

Frustratingly, the only option.

'We've got West county and Kent on alert too, sir.'

But this was Cartier they were seeking.

Then the phone again: for me.

'My dear, there is something else that is happening! I do not know, but I think it is best you should be told.'

'What is it?'

132

'There comes this taxi with another Frenchman, known to the others. I cannot hear what, but they are very excited, and at once go out to the two cars.'

'They've gone?'

'Aha. But this time I run out in the street to see which way. They turn to the right, and, later, to the left, as though they are going the way we went yesterday.'

In fact, towards the coast – were the comrades on the scent too?

'I'll be right with you.'

To Ringmer I said: 'A blue Citroen BX and a white Renault 21 – alert the patrols for them too. I'll be listening out for the reports.'

Ringmer said: 'Oh Lord – is that lot on the loose too?'

'Going towards the coast,' I said. 'And their guess is probably better than ours.'

Better than ours: as I slammed out of the car park, Gabrielle gave me the details.

'This man I think they are expecting, because they leave the pork-butcher waiting in reception. The others have gone into the little lounge, where they sit about saying not very much. It is my impression that they have plans ready laid and await only the arrival of this man.'

'They hadn't booked out?'

'Oh no, my friend. At least, they bring down no luggage. And long they have not to wait before this taxi pulls up at the door. The man who gets out is of an age with the others, lean, sharp-featured, with bushy grey hair, and clearly he is well-known to the pork-butcher, who hastens to embrace him and kiss his cheeks. Then the pork-butcher puts his finger to his lips and hastens the man through to the little lounge, where, like an employee to his boss, he mutters some message to Monsieur Brezolles. The rest hang around listening, and then – *vite, vite!* The poor man has not time to check even his bag. One and all they run out to the cars, and drive away as I have said.'

133

'Their plans were made. They knew the messenger was coming.'

'Of that, I would say, small doubt. Can it be they have information about the shopkeeper?'

'That's the guess. There has been a leak.'

'A leak, yes.' She nodded her head. 'And with the comrades no surprise, my friend, for they have ears in every department.'

'They will know about Cartier. And, it seems, the rendezvous.'

Gabrielle looked grave. 'I do not know. At times I am feeling even sorry for that shopkeeper, who, however, can deserve little pity.'

I cleared the town impatiently and drove fast towards Southhaven. We were at least twenty minutes behind the two French cars, but, against that, the drivers were unfamiliar with the country. For them, a remote location would probably mean sessions with a map, and the chances were that we might catch up with them in some garage forecourt or layby. The switched-on transceiver stayed silent. Traffic was Sunday-morning light. The one car we did happen on in a layby was a police patrol Escort. I hauled up and identified myself.

'Have either the Metro or the French cars gone by?'

'Not while I've been here, sir. But I've only just arrived from Sudbourne.'

'Stick with them if you see them. And call in at once.'

Had they turned off already? I tried to flick the map through my mind, but to the best of my memory the sideroads led only to populous villages. And always it was possible they hadn't taken this way at all: the turn Gabrielle had seen the two cars make gave other options than the coast. I drove on more warily, slowing to stare into junctions, at sign-boards. Southhaven was arriving, and the superstructure of the ferry which had probably decanted the messenger that morning.

'It cannot be to the ferryport that they go?'

134

And suddenly, it didn't seem improbable. The charter-plane at Lydd, like the rented Montego, could well have been a bait to catch fools. I put on speed again, into the town, into the slot outside the AA. Cars were already forming queues, but among them not the three I was seeking. I accosted the dock-policeman on point.

'Last night's alert – it is still on?'

'Yes, sir. We have the man's description.'

'He may now be accompanied by a Frenchman in his forties, six foot, heavy build, dark hair and striking blue eyes. They may be on foot or in a dun-coloured Metro, and the wanted man may now have false papers. Any sign of them?'

'No sir. They haven't come this way yet.'

'Also, a blue Citroen BX with four men in their sixties, accompanied by a white Renault 21 with two men and a woman.'

'Don't think I've seen them, sir, but I couldn't be certain.'

'If you do, ring Leyhurst at once.'

Worth a try; but I was beginning to feel that I was barking up wrong trees. The action was going on somewhere else, and my only clue a bum one. I stared for a moment at the ferry, at the cars, now beginning to creep towards the ramp. If I were Cartier, where . . .? But only the yelping gulls answered me.

'We are out of luck, my dear.'

I drifted the Rover back out of town. In front of me, the whole of East Sussex, and, when I'd done with that, Kent. It wasn't on. I slid the car into a layby and flipped the transceiver.

'Any sightings yet?'

'Half a mo, sir . . . something's coming in now. What's your position, sir?'

'Southhaven.'

'We've got a possible sighting at Maynard's Corner. Two cars answering the description seen passing by the junction, but our man couldn't be sure. He was attending an accident down the road.'

'Heading which way?'

'Towards Bawdsey, sir. That's only a mile or two from you.'

Yes it was. Yes it was. I hoiked the Rover out of the layby. Bawdsey. Bawdsey Head. Where better for Cartier to play his games? I drove fast, overtaking, slowing only for Bawdsey's few houses, slammed into the lane, barely a road, that wriggled its way towards the sea. And then:

'Aha – we find them all!'

The blue Citroen. The white Renault. The dun-coloured Metro. And seven people standing round them: not one of whom was Cartier.

I bumped the Rover across the turf to park well short of the group. Today there wasn't even a haze on the Channel, stretching greyly from somewhere below. Perfect sun was lighting the scene, a perfect breeze caressed it. And the seven people stood quite still, watching me walk towards them. I pointed to the Metro.

'Where's the driver?'

They stared at me, said nothing.

'I require an answer. Where's the driver?'

'Monsieur,' Brezolles faltered. 'We do not know. The driver of the car is not with us, we arrive to find it already parked here.'

'Then you park beside it?'

'By chance only, monsieur. Our business here is purely pleasure. On a fine day, a small outing to divert the mind of madame from her sorrow.'

I gazed at him. 'No, monsieur.'

'Monsieur?'

'We both know who was driving that car. Also who he had come here to meet, and what his probable intentions were. So where is he – and more to the point, where is the man he came to meet?'

136

Brezolles tried to make his face a blank. 'You amaze me, monsieur. I repeat, we come here entirely for pleasure, having been joined this morning, at my invitation, by my friend and colleague, the good Monsieur Logny.'

'Who brought you a message.'

'Indeed. That the affairs of our firm need not my presence.'

'Whereupon you at once drive to this spot?'

He shrugged and went on staring blankly.

'Oh, for shame, monsieur!' Gabrielle broke in. 'Do not waste time with such foolish lies. Meanwhile it may be that the driver of that car is spiriting away the man we seek. He has an aeroplane waiting, ha? And all the time ships are sailing for France. You will cooperate with monsieur my husband if you wish to spit on Darlan's face.'

'Madame, I am at a loss –'

'In the eye of a pig! Monsieur, I am witness of what happened this morning. That gentleman there brought a message, yes, but it dealt not with pettifoggings in Evreux. Oh no, it is from the comrades to tell you what shall happen at this spot, and into your cars you go at once, and here we find you by an empty car. And so? And so?'

'Madame –'

'You are near arrest, monsieur, for obstruction.'

Brezolles flung his hands in a gesture, turned helplessly to the others.

'Tell him, Bertrand.'

Madame Bernay took a step closer to the lawyer.

'But, dear Simone –'

'Tell him. I, too, am tired of taking shelter in lies. This is not Pierre's way, ha? Not the way of men who are men. And it is true that the traitor Darlan may at this moment be escaping. So speak to the man.'

Another gesture. Then Brezolles turned with out-stretched hand:

'Monsieur, some truth, a very little, may be in the allegations of madame, your wife. Some rumours, shall we say, have reached us that a certain rendezvous here was imminent. Thus, though strictly in the interests of justice, we felt our duty was to be present, to ensure, if the danger existed, that a wanted man should not escape.'

Madame Bernay spat.

'Go on,' I said.

'Alas, monsieur, we are too late. We arrive, as formerly I said, to find only this empty car, and we conjecture that the two men have departed in another car, to perfect their arrangements. Then monsieur appears.'

'You saw another car?'

'But distantly, monsieur. It is leaving the lane as we approach.'

'But you can describe it?'

Brezolles shrugged. 'It is driving away from us, and soon lost. But the colour is that one describes as beige and the car, I think, is an estate.'

'Wait here – all of you.'

I hurried back to the Rover, jumped in and flicked the transceiver.

'I'm on the cliff-top at Bawdsey. Cartier has dumped his car here. Madame Bernay and her friends are here and saw a car leaving that answers the description of Caudry's.'

'Could they give a direction, sir?'

'East from Bawdsey village. And it can't have been gone more than half an hour.'

'Received and understood, sir.'

'And you can send me some back-up.'

I returned to the group by the cars, to be accosted at once by Madame Bernay.

'Monsieur, our information you have, and we request to be allowed to go on our way.'

I shook my head. 'You will remain here. The capture of Caudry is the business of the police.'

138

Her eyes were fierce. 'If we choose to go, monsieur, neither yourself nor your wife shall stop us. It may have been, but for your interference, that the traitor Darlan would yet have returned here.'

'You must remain here.'

'Ha. Why?'

'Let us say to give statements to the police when they come.'

Her eyes were explosive for a moment and then, it was inevitable, she spat.

With their eyes on me, I approached the Metro, though without expecting to learn much from it. I tried the door, found it unlocked, and noticed the keys still in the ignition. So what had happened here, in this lonely place, witnessed only by the panorama of the sea: when Greek had met Greek, beige estate by mud-coloured Metro? Their time together had not been long. At the most, they could have talked for about twenty minutes: enough for Caudry to have blabbed, if he'd been fool enough, but not to have made his written statement. So then? A removal elsewhere, Caudry driving, and perhaps with a gun on him. Or had he been so unwise as to bring a statement with him, to have it wrested from him . . . also at gun-point?

I stared at the turf about the car: no blood, but there was something else: a welt cut out by the heel of a shoe, the shoe of someone reacting with violence. I looked further. The turf was short, springy, unapt to receive impressions. But one there was. A triangular drag-mark. And then another. And a third. I didn't have to track them. Straight and true, they were pointing to the cliff-edge. I strode across, stood looking down into that cavern of space. To the gulls. The breakers.

'Just stay back!'

In my car I carried glasses, and I ran across to fetch them. Gabrielle had moved a few steps towards the cliff-edge, the others stood silent where they were. I trained the glasses on what I had seen: the bundle being pushed and dragged by

139

the sea, the heavy bundle, sodden, dark, where the gulls were most yelling. The sea rolled it. Displayed it. I looked, then put my glasses away.

Gabrielle said: 'It is – him?'

I shook my head.

'Cartier.'

10

The back-up, two uniform-men, arrived at that moment, and I set them to guard the Metro, the tracks, while I called my message in. I got Ringmer.

'We need a launch round at once. The tide may shift the body.'

'You're certain of who it is, sir?'

'Yes. He was overpowered, dumped over.'

'Holy Jesus! And Moossoo did that?'

'That's the immediate assumption.'

'I never thought he had it in him, sir. It just goes to show.'

Or . . . did it? I stalked back to the French party, who now had drawn together in a close group: the seven from Evreux: madame, her brother, the Musketeers and the shifty-eyed late-comer. I stared at each one.

'Well?'

Not even Brezolles ventured to answer.

I said: 'You gave me a tale about a vanishing estate-car.'

Brezolles faltered: 'But it was true, monsieur . . .'

'Either true or extremely convenient.'

'All is exactly as we told it! We arrive here to find a deserted car.'

'You could equally well have found it with the driver. A man whose intentions were well-known to you. That interfered with your own. And who may have threatened you with a gun.'

'But that is not so!'

'Monsieur,' I said. 'Walk with me to that cliff-edge.'

For an instant, fear in his eyes. Then he drew himself up, and we walked, stared down into the murmurous void.

'So?'

'I think . . . a bundle . . .'

'That bundle is a body, monsieur.'

'But I did not know . . . we have not the knowledge . . . monsieur! Whose body is that down there?'

I stared hard. 'The body of a man who would not easily be overcome. A man familiar with danger. And who was alert to his danger here.'

'It is – Darlan?'

I said nothing.

'Monsieur, believe me, we know nothing of this! The truth has been told, we are lately arrived, we find only the deserted car.'

'I repeat, that man would not be easily overcome.'

'But you cannot suspect that we – ?'

'It is more credible, monsieur, than that a single opponent is responsible for what happened here.'

'Oh monsieur, monsieur!' He rocked his shoulders. 'I am a lawyer, I understand. It is the logic, it is more probable, but, monsieur, it is not the truth. We find no one. We are not threatened. We toss nobody over the cliff. Should an unlawful act have been proceeding, we would at once have intervened.'

'You were here to deal with Darlan.'

'Perhaps, to arrest him.'

'Then your information should have gone to the police.'

'Let us say, we are not sure –'

I made a gesture of disgust.

Brezolles wrung his hands.

'So?'

'Monsieur has the advantage. He knows the identity of that man down there. If, indeed, it is the traitor Darlan, then, may I say, justice has been done. But – is it Darlan?'

I kept staring.

'Monsieur, it is vital, do you not see? For then the hour has struck, all is ending here, and the martyrs of Trouville have been avenged. Please, will you not tell me?'

I merely shrugged. Perhaps the body would be more informative. I was seeing, down towards Southhaven, the black dot, the spray-feather of the approaching police launch. Meanwhile the tide must have been on the ebb, since only the odd breaker was rolling the body.

'We shall require statements from each one of you.'

'Monsieur, I think that body cannot be Darlan's. I see now that it has dark hair, while the hair of the traitor must surely be grey.'

'Your own hair, monsieur, is strangely black.'

'But it has not been soaking in the sea. No, no, monsieur. That man is the agent, and Darlan, once more, has slipped through our fingers.'

Fresh cars were arriving. I went to meet them, left Brezolles to report to his anxious crew. Gabrielle had gone back to stand by the Rover, was staring wretchedly at the grey sea.

The launch brought him into a dock at Southhaven; Ringmer had Praed standing by. The body was carted into a storeshed used by fishermen and laid out on boxes covered with old nets. We got his clothes off. He'd been wearing a gun, but all we found was the empty holster; and the launch-crew had combed the beach area without turning up the weapon.

'If chummie wasn't armed before . . .'

The sloppy jacket was a storehouse. Tucked away in several pockets was the gear to provide a fresh identity – a French birth-certificate and passport, in the name of Louis Legrand, together with a miniature polaroid camera and an embossing tool for the completion of the passport. Ammunition too and a wad of notes – the killer had been in too much of a hurry.

'I wasn't really believing this, sir, till now.'

143

'Cartier came prepared to lift Caudry out.'

'There's a couple of grand here at least. And these docs would have got past the check at Lydd.'

Meanwhile, Praed:

'If you want an opinion, this man was dead when he struck the ground. Another blunt-instrument victim. But this time, a different weapon.'

'Can you give us a guess?'

'A guess only, mind you. It would be some manner of iron bar. What we have is a similar depressed fracture, but in this case long and relatively narrow.'

'The handle of a car-jack?'

'That would fit. Provided it was one of the solid kind.'

Ringmer shook his head. 'I can't figure this! Chummie must have been laying for him when he got there. Yet he was doing just what chummie was asking, so why would chummie act like that?'

'Caudry knows the game. He may have spotted something that told him Cartier had other intentions.'

'And then he goes to his car for a jack-handle?'

I hunched: I wasn't getting it either.

'Caudry didn't trust him. He was having second thoughts. That's why he's been trying to contact us. Then somehow Cartier makes a slip, and, before he can protect himself, Caudry attacks him.'

'Before he can pull his gun, even?'

'Unless he confesses, we may never know what happened.'

Praed said: 'What you are dealing with is clearly a man in the acute stage of paranoia. At the faintest suspicion of hostile intent he is likely to respond with irrational violence. It may be only that the victim refused him a cigarette, or merely looked at him in a certain way. That would be enough for him to kill in his present state of mind.'

Ringmer gazed at him. 'You mean he's flipped completely?'

'If that's the way you care to put it.'

'Oh lord. And now he's loose with a gun.'

'Then the moral is extremely plain.'

'You bet it is!'

'Wait,' I said. 'We don't know what happened on the cliff-top. If Cartier tried to use that gun, then Caudry's response was scarcely irrational. I've talked to Caudry. Caudry is a man with terrible things on his conscience. Certainly paranoid, but scarcely irrational. Survival is first and last his signature.'

'So he'd blast a policeman.'

I shook my head. 'We're his fall-back option, remember? Unless we push him into a corner I doubt whether he would use the gun on us. That's for his Resistance colleagues if they get to him first, but us he has to talk to. We're his last chance, now.'

Ringmer looked doubtful. 'So what do we do?'

'In the first place, we avoid a shoot-out. He's in the district, if we find him, lay off, and hear what he has to say.'

'And if we don't find him?'

'He'll find us. Sooner or later, that phone will ring.'

'It'll come to someone going in, sir. Empty-handed.'

'Then that someone will be me.'

Ringmer stared. Praed said:

'Well, you have my opinion of the matter. If such things were available for use on human subjects, I would advise a tranquillising dart. At least, the officer should be given cover, with a pre-emptive strike in mind.'

'No guns,' I said.

'Then the likelihood is that I shall have another post-mortem on my hands.'

A tight-faced Scot, he left his instructions about the body, and went. Ringmer stared puzzledly at the body, now draped with a couple of sacks.

'I don't know, sir,' he said. 'But there's a lot of sense in what he says. I'd be happier with guns. And we don't

145

have to use them.'

'We want Caudry alive, don't we?'

'Yes, of course! But just the same. And the C.C. may order guns anyway.'

I shrugged; I'd done my best. 'Is there still cover at the shop?'

'Yes sir.'

I went out of that shed, back to the Rover, to Gabrielle. Behind me, the ferry was just pulling away, gave wailing toots on its siren.

'It is suddenly so sad, my dear. And not because that man is dead.'

She had been silent until now, a withdrawn expression on her pretty face. I hadn't known her like this before. It was as though some vital thing had died in her: and I felt anger. Anger because these events, in the present and from the past, had thrown this veil on my Gabrielle.

'One can't feel emotion for Cartier. He was a man beyond pity.'

'Not him. Not anyone. And yet, perhaps, for all of them.'

'All of them?'

'How shall I say? They are each one caught in this terrible web. Because something happens so long ago, with other people, in other times. But now, already, two dead, and the web still tight about the others. And nothing will break this, will let them go. It is terrible and it is sad.'

'Crime works that way.'

'You say.'

'These people are involved because they choose it.'

'I do not know. I am seeing it different. As though a play which some bad person is writing.'

'Only each one is writing his own script – Caudry, Cartier, the rest.'

'Then, it is under compulsion they write.'

'In that case, who compels them?'

146

It didn't quite get a smile, but she relaxed a little, touched my knee. I set the Rover in motion and we drove away from the docks, the shed. I switched on the transceiver. Messages were going through from patrols who hadn't sighted Caudry. Clearly he had gone to earth . . . but where? East Sussex had never seemed so large.

'Is it that we too are still searching?'

'Not now. We've lost our ferret. And now that Caudry has a gun things have taken a different complexion.'

'And so?'

'He wants to talk, but my fear is that he'll never be allowed to.' I gave her a glance. 'I'm probably superfluous. If you've changed your mind, we can still leave.'

She stared frowningly ahead. 'Is it not to you he wishes to speak?'

'That was the message. But if I learn his position, I shall be obliged to pass it on.'

'And then they go in with guns?'

'It's their case. Not mine.'

'Yet – still some good you can do?'

'Just at the moment, it seems marginal.'

'But yes. At the moment.' Her hand grasped my knee. 'Yet, all this time, things are happening quickly, and who knows the events of the next hour? Two men have died in this bad play, it may be our chance to prevent a third – and so, no, no, my friend! Still we shall see it through to the end. He will be on the phone, you think, the shopkeeper?'

'He has twice rung the shop.'

'Then, at the shop we shall wait, you and I, and perhaps the third time is lucky.'

'I can't give him any promises.'

'That we shall see. A plan, it may be, will rear its head. But first we must talk to this fearful creature, and that is what we will do.'

I pressed her hand. 'Then you are still a brave girl.'

'Attend to your driving, my friend, if you please. You are forgetting that these things are French matters, though played out in your pleasant land.'

I struck the road back to Leyhurst and drove. Still the abortive messages were going through. One patrol had spotted a beige estate in a farmyard, only to nick a most indignant pig-dealer.

The gates of Caudry's yard were unlocked, and after a moment's thought I parked the car inside. The warehouse door was opened promptly by a relieved-looking D.C.

'I thought I was stuck here for the day, sir. They say there's no one spare to give me a break.'

'I'll take over now.'

'Yes sir. Nor I didn't know how to contact you, anyway.'

'Caudry hasn't rung?'

'Oh no, sir. I've been twiddling my thumbs in there. But there's milk in the fridge and I made some tea – I didn't think chummie was going to mind.'

'On your way back, call in at the hotel and ask them to send over some sandwiches.'

He gave me his key, and left. We braved the odour of sheepskin and entered. Gabrielle pushed through to the gloomy shop, outside which the sunny street appeared dazzling. There, twenty-four hours since, almost to the minute, we'd seen Caudry serving his last customer, most likely his very last: the final sale of forty years. Already that shop was posthumous, had an air of vacancy about it.

'Never can he come back, my friend.'

No. Though he rode every charge we threw at him. Witness the white Renault creeping by to make its turn into the hotel car park.

'For so long he lives here, following his trade, doing no harm to any person. At last, when the shop stays shut, they are finding him dead where always he has lived. Or so it would have been until comes this tourist, out of all of

148

France, one, when, in a moment, he is a fugitive, killing men in order to stay alive.'

'Because he was not that innocent man, keeping his shop in the High Street.'

'But yes. Until that moment. Between when he is a young man and when he is growing old. First he is a vile creature, then, for many years, a funny Frenchman who the English adore, and now, again, forced to be the vile creature, because, long ago, it is how he began. Then which man shall we say he is?'

'Both one and the other.'

'Ha. It is not the logic, my friend. He is not two men, but one, and that is the very great sadness.'

'Let's go upstairs.'

If the shop was gloomy, the flat was haunted by the presence of the dead woman, she whose photograph on the dressing-table was still surrounded by feminine trinkets. Indeed Caudry had apparently been using the spare bedroom, a bleak little cell overlooking the yard, leaving the connubial chamber, untouched, to the manes of the departed. The fussy furniture in the lounge was hers, the sentimental pictures of dogs and children, and, in the kitchen, the flower-pattern crockery that lined a dresser. And all was clean and tidy: except the D.C.'s cup and saucer in the sink.

'Except for the poor little bedroom, one could not tell that a man lived here. At any moment, that lady in the photograph could be walking in to demand our business.'

'She has been dead several years.'

'But see, in the drawers, in the wardrobe, her clothes. It is eerie, yes? It is as though he were the ghost, and she the living.'

'Perhaps that's how it was.'

'How it was . . .?'

'He was living the life of a ghost. A pretence life, based on a reality that couldn't be spoken.'

'But the lady, she was real.'

'Yes.'

Gabrielle gave a little shiver.

A clue could there be in that forlorn place? Ringmer's search had not been the most thorough. Yet so little there was of Caudry's, so much of the dead wife's. I sorted through the bureau in the lounge, where Malling had found the sister's letters; the best I could turn up was a bunch of old travel brochures, offering holidays in Germany and Spain. A hint there? But they'd belonged to the wife, were included in a drawer with knitting-patterns. I moved on to the small bedroom, and there, at last, found something that set my nostrils twitching.

'See here.'

In a battered box-file, some recent literature from an estate-agent; the details of five coastal properties, bungalows with such names as 'Seaholme' and 'Wavecrest'.

'He has bought a property, you are thinking?'

'He has to be somewhere. And that somewhere is in the district. Half an hour after he was spotted at Bawdsey, the patrols were searching for him in vain.'

'Aha – because he buys a hideaway!'

'Hand me that telephone directory.'

The name of the agent was Simon Rutger. Surprisingly, four 'Rutger, S.' entries were listed, but I got my man at the second attempt.

'You are the estate-agent?'

'Yes, I am. But I don't do business on a Sunday –'

'This is a police enquiry. Among your clients, do you have a Jean Caudry, with an address in Leyhurst?'

'Hold on – that rings a bell. Is he the Frenchman at The Camping Shop?'

'That's him.'

'Well, he isn't a client, though we've shown him over a couple of properties. He was looking for something cheap and cheerful, preferably off the beaten track.'

'When was this?'

'Oh, last year at this time. Autumn is when the punters are selling. He saw a property he fancied in the *Argus* and gave us a ring. But it came to nothing.'

'Would you know if he was suited by one of your colleagues?'

'Couldn't tell you that off-hand. But look, what's this all about?'

'Thank you for your assistance, Mr. Rutger.'

I'd tilted the phone so that Gabrielle could hear: now she was staring with solemn eyes.

'So – we can find him! It is a matter only of ringing the colleagues of Mr. Rutger.'

I made a face. 'Only is right. This just happens to be a Sunday. All their offices are closed, and they themselves may be from home.'

'But, if we cannot, then the good Ringmer, with numerous men and local knowledge?'

For a moment I was tempted; then I withdrew my hand from the phone. Tell Ringmer, and tooled-up policemen would surround that 'Seaholme' or 'Beach View'.

'Somehow, we have to talk to him first.'

'But, if he does not soon ring?'

'We'll wait. Right at this time, he may be finding it tricky to get to a phone.'

And even as I spoke the phone rang: I lifted it to hear the ringing-signal of a call-box.

'Chief Superintendent Gently.'

At first, all I could discern was rough breathing. I slipped a ballpen from my pocket, scribbled 'Caudry' on the margin of Rutger's property list. Gabrielle took the pen to write 'I go to ring police?', but I shook my head, scribbled 'No.'

'Caudry?'

More of the breathing!

'You can talk to me, Caudry. I'm on my own.'

Behind the breathing, now more controlled, was it the sound of surf I could faintly hear?

151

'Caudry!'

'Monsieur . . . is it truly yourself?'

'I've been waiting here for your call, Caudry.'

'Monsieur, they are everywhere, it is not easy. And doubtless you are tracing this call, yes?'

'No, Caudry. You can talk. I shall not have this call traced. But let me tell you, we have found Cartier. And we are not treating it as an accident.'

'Cartier, monsieur? I do not know –'

'Listen, Caudry! We talk straight. I know of the deal you had with Cartier, and I know the sort of man he was. What happened?'

'I admit nothing, monsieur – '

'Then let me tell you where you stand. The police see you now as an armed killer who is to be hunted down with guns. If they catch you, little chance of a dialogue. Your best chance is here and now.'

'But I have no gun, monsieur – '

'Don't lie!'

'Oh monsieur, if only you knew! At once I realise I am making a mistake in revealing myself to our intelligence.'

'You being formerly Darlan the traitor.'

'That man is dead – '

'Don't waste your lies!'

'Please, monsieur, please! I will not admit this. But you may take it so if you choose.'

'I do so choose. It fetched Cartier running.'

'I am telling him a tale, just a tale, monsieur. I am hunted by the police, by the vengeful comrades, I seek only the means to save my life.'

'You are saying you had no information to sell him?'

'Perhaps a little – a very little! Enough, it may be, for our intelligence to give me assistance, sorely needed. But I am a fool, yes, to trust these people, who, when they have sucked oranges, throw them away. Yet the comrades were here, I had seen them, and to the rendezvous I must go.'

'So – what happened?'

'I save my life only! That man has certainly come there to kill me. I am prepared, yes? As he alights from the car, his jacket falls back, and I am seeing a gun.'

'And you – you were armed?'

'But yes. In my sleeve is a poker, it matters not from where. At once it is sliding down into my hand, and, before he can straighten up, the deed is done.'

'And then – over the cliff.'

'Like a dead dog, monsieur.'

'Pausing only to take his gun.'

'What would monsieur have? On all sides I am threatened. For the comrades are arriving as I drive away.'

'Self-defence.'

'Am I not saying?'

'And self-defence again when you killed Bernay?'

At which point the coin ran out, and there were scufflings at the other end, and finally a clang.

'Monsieur, I admit nothing about that – he is killed in the storm, may we not agree?'

'We may not, Caudry. The proof is in our hands. A full confession is the only deal.'

'But, monsieur – !'

I said: 'This is the offer, and if you want to stay alive you had better take it. A written confession to both killings, and lying on top of it, Cartier's gun. You'll be dealing with me. I shall arrest you personally. I will take all steps to assure your safety. In return for your confession it may just be that the police will act generously with your case. Do I make myself plain?'

'I admit nothing, monsieur!'

'One thing more. You haven't long to decide. We have a clue now to where you are hiding, and soon you may find yourself facing a shoot-out.'

'Monsieur, I do not trust you.'

'I'm your best hope, Caudry. If you're wise, you'll accept the deal.'

153

'I lay down the gun, yes, but, ha, ha, what shall happen then?'

'Don't act like a fool.'

'Oh no. Oh no. I shall not act like a fool, monsieur. I am to confess what I do not admit, and then I shall give you the gun, too?'

'That's the deal. Now tell me where to reach you.'

'Already on this telephone I am too long. Once, I am thinking I can trust you, monsieur, but, no longer. You are one with the rest.'

'Think about it, Caudry. Ring me back.'

But he had hung up before I'd finished speaking. Gabrielle, who had caught snatches on the tilted phone, gave an exasperated exclamation.

'So! Then he wishes to die. By himself he judges all others. You will now call the good Ringmer, ha, and set him upon the scent of this madman?'

Once more I was tempted. But didn't.

'We must give him a chance to think it over.'

'My friend, it will do no good. That man speaking there had doom in his voice. Moreover, if the police do not shoot him, there are those not so very far behind.'

She nodded to the window: down below, outside the hotel, sat the blue Citroen; and the faces of the men inside it were turned towards the flat.

'They are not fools, and they have their intelligence. So soon they were snapping at Cartier's heels! They, too, know the shopkeeper is at no great distance, and have now a description of his car. Bear in mind they are men of the Resistance, who, before today, may have smoked out foxes.'

Before I could reply the phone range again: I grabbed it up. Ringmer.

'There's someone here who wants to see you, sir. Says he comes from the Yard, and not to bother with names.'

'A man. What man?'

The phone was handed over.

'Hullo, old man,' a voice said. 'Exit Cartier, and enter me.'

Now, the Special Branch was amongst us.

11

'He is the officer who, in Scotland, was thrown out of a hotel by the excellent Sinclair?'

I nodded. 'Chief Superintendent Empton. What's happened to Cartier has brought him running.'

'And that is bad?'

'Very bad for Caudry. His chances are lessening by the minute.'

'Aha. I recall him now. A man, you say, as ruthless as he who is dead.'

Just as ruthless; and probably cleverer. A man depended on for results. And who would have guessed first time, if the grape-vine hadn't told him, what Cartier's business had been with Caudry.

'What, then, shall we do?'

I shook my head. The final act of the tragedy had simply come closer. Now, even if Caudry came to his senses, the time for intervention had almost run out.

'You cannot talk to this man?'

'To Empton?'

'At least, he must be wishing for the shopkeeper alive.'

'Alive until he talks. After that, as with Cartier, it is his silence that becomes appropriate.'

'But if all along the shopkeeper has lied, my friend, and does not truly have this information?'

'Then he's lied himself into his grave.'

'Yet, if your Empton could be made to believe this?'

I paused. We stared at each other; I had talked to Caudry,

I had talked to him lately. Just possible I could pull that one on Empton? If so, I'd deserve a gold medal.

'He wouldn't go away.'

'But you try, ha? A little time it could be buying. And then you are arresting the shopkeeper, and keeping him out of your Empton's hands.'

I stared some more. 'There's an outside chance. But only if Caudry is ready to confess. And ready to trust me.'

'Then go, my friend. Leave me. I will remain beside the telephone. You shall talk foolishness to your Empton, and I, perhaps, reason to the shopkeeper.'

I went, shaking my head. The men in the Citroen stared as I passed. Outside the police station, another car, a black Jaguar with personalised plates. The two men in it also stared: Empton's jackals, Curtis and Meaker. Ringmer was hovering in reception.

'You know this fellow, do you, sir? He's waiting in the office, says he wants a word with you alone.'

'I know him.'

'I was a bit insubordinate. He came swanning in here like he owned Sussex. Told me shooters were out if we found Moossoo, and that a few dead policemen didn't count.'

'That's running to form. Pay no attention.'

'All the same I was wanting to kick him.'

Which was Empton's usual effect on people. I went in at the office without knocking.

The smell of Russian cigarettes is the smell of Empton and that was the smell in Ringmer's office. He sat sprawled on Ringmer's chair, his feet on the desk, mouthing grey smoke rings towards the ceiling. He blew one at me.

'Close the door, old man. I've checked for bugs, and there aren't any. So we can exchange a few words of wisdom before you hit the trail back to the metropolis.'

A lean six feet, hawkish features, eyes of a paler blue than Cartier's: dressed in a sharkskin twopiece with a Tattersall check shirt and mauve bow-tie.

157

'What do you want, Empton?'

'Hear him ask me! You've been a naughty boy, old man. Playing with the frogs has got to be a habit. Which, between us, you're going to have to break. Was it you who took Cartier out, by the way?'

I didn't even bother to give him the eye. I hooked a chair across and took a seat towards the end of the desk where his feet weren't. He removed the feet.

'Another little habit! These unofficial dealings with the ungodly. Just like those rainy days in Scotland. I hear you're at it again, sonny-boy.'

'So what do you want?'

'Such impatience. And Cartier barely cold. You had words with him before he went.' His pale eyes were tight. 'What did you get?'

I said: 'That he was here on a fool's errand.'

'Doesn't sound like Cartier, old man.'

I said: 'You can fool even Cartiers if you use the right bait.'

'And the right bait?'

'Hot info.'

'Yes,' Empton said. 'Yes. Hot info. From a bird like Caudry. Alias Darlan. What could it have been?'

'Caudry wanted out. He offered a deal. To name collaborators in high office. He named a minister off the cuff. It was a deal the French couldn't refuse.'

'So interesting,' Empton said. 'Who was the minister he mentioned?'

'Cartier didn't say.'

'But lots of others?'

'Doubtless Caudry laid it on with a trowel.'

'He would do, wouldn't he,' Empton said. 'And you went along with this cheesy deal?'

'Cartier promised to play by the book, but then fooled us with the rendezvous.'

'Ah yes,' Empton said. 'The cliff-top gambol. What exactly did happen there, old man? An old hand like

158

Cartier, too. And not known for his chumminess with certain people.'

'Caudry didn't trust him.'

'So wise.'

'Caudry didn't have the names to deliver. He carried a poker up his sleeve, saw Cartier's gun and attacked him.'

'Should stand up in court,' Empton said. 'So long as Caudry doesn't swear different.'

'This is Caudry's account,' I said.

'Ah,' Empton said. 'Now it does get interesting.' He lit a fresh cigarette from the stub of the first, blew smoke in my general direction. 'So where is he,' he said. 'This ingenious frog. Who spills his guts to my least-favourite person?'

'He rang me.'

'Oh, please,' Empton said.

'He wants to come in from the cold.'

'So where is he?'

'Somewhere out there.'

Empton drew a lungful and exhaled it viciously.

'My dear little man,' he said. 'Between us and these four walls. There are men up there, very high up there, who want that info out of his entrails. Deals are going on with the frogs and the frogs are tricksy, handle needed. Caudry has it, and they know he has it. Just him going through our hands is enough.'

'Going through your hands.'

'Not a mark on him.'

'I saw Meaker and Curtis outside.'

'Old man, you know my kindly nature. Nothing they can't limp away from afterwards. We'll talk to him like his uncle, him with Cartier on his conscience. Gentle persuasion to see it our way. Then the video and the signed statement.'

'And then?'

Empton formed a careful ring. 'A little reunion seems to be the drill. With those pals of his who infest the town. Must

159

let the peasants have their bread and circuses. So. Where is he?'

'Still out there.'

'But talking deals to the kind man.'

I said: 'I tried to do a deal, but Caudry's trusting no one just now.'

'Come on,' Empton said. 'Rules and all, you'd get something out of a chat. Like where the wollies should start in. Where little froggie was making his call.'

'A call from a box. Untraced. A deal to give himself up. To go easy on him for the killings. He thought I was conning and hung up.'

'Yeah,' Empton said. 'Yeah. Never mind about the killings. Those two frogs died in accidents and that's official, old man.'

'Except one he confessed to.'

'Nerves,' Empton said.

'And the other we can prove.'

'Pomade on a mallet,' Empton said. 'The wollie told me. And me going to find pomade in Caudry's boudoir.'

I stared at him, shook my head. 'He's wanted for murder by this authority. He'll be held here. Interrogated here. And always in the presence of senior officers.'

'Not now,' Empton said. 'Didn't you hear me? Frog one was killed by a falling tree. Frog two slipped his foot and fell over a cliff. Which leaves just me wanting Caudry's company.'

'You won't get away with it.'

'Tut, old man. And me here with full authority.'

'In any case Caudry's info is suspect.'

'Oh dear,' Empton said. 'If the frogs only knew that.' He puffed, stubbed out the cigarette. 'Now let's have it on the table. You're just a nuisance here, old man, unwanted, unofficial and a pain in my arse. Me, I'm official. I was sent here. I've got a job. I mean to do it. And if it's outside Magna Carta what a shame. But it gets done.' He leaned across the desk. 'And I don't trust you, old man. You've held out on

160

your uncle before. And if you're holding out on me now that's just too bad. Better up your insurance.'

I just stared.

'Where's Caudry?'

'If I knew, I would inform this authority.'

'Yeah,' Empton said. 'This authority. Who as of now are working with me. So you tell them?'

'I don't know.'

'Don't know,' Empton said. 'And I have to believe it. And like that you become superfluous, chase your tail back to London.'

I shook my head. 'I stay.'

'Then keep watching it,' Empton said. 'Your back.'

A knock on the door was Ringmer.

'Sir, a possible sighting of the car – '

'Hold it,' Empton snapped. 'Our friend is leaving. This is information for the men.'

'Sir – ?'

'Do what he says,' I said. 'But before I go you need to hear this. Caudry rang. He confessed to killing Cartier, wasn't yet ready to confess to the other. But for that we have hard evidence, so both charges can go ahead. In Cartier's case, the weapon was a poker. Caudry is very nervous, but probably ready to surrender.'

Empton snarled: 'He didn't hear that!'

'He heard it,' I said. 'And so did you. Caudry is answerable to the East Sussex Constabulary, in whose authority the crimes were committed.'

'My authority pre-empts theirs!'

'Not in a case of murder. And any interrogation by you will be carried out under their auspices.'

Ringmer was goggling. 'But, sir – !'

'I'll get you for this,' Empton snarled. 'Foul me up and your feet won't touch. You'll be suspended before you can spit.'

I said to Ringmer: 'One last thing. Did you find any pomade when you searched Caudry's flat?'

'Pomade? No, sir.'

'And neither did I. Let's both remember that, shall we?'

I got out. Empton was foaming. The goons in his car gave me hard looks. But I didn't go very far; something else I'd seen: the blue Citroen, lurking in a side-road. I stepped into a doorway. I hadn't long to wait. Empton, Ringmer and side-kicks came out to the cars. The black Jaguar swept away, followed by a police Granada: followed, at a distance, by the Citroen.

Had the sighting been positive? I couldn't know. But surely the end wasn't far away. It was a miracle that Caudry had escaped for so long, out there in whatever last refuge he had run to.

The white Renault had replaced the Citroen in the slot in front of the hotel, and now it was Madame Bernay's black eyes that watched my every step as I passed by. No point in evasion: I went straight through the doors into the yard. But, before rejoining Gabrielle, I got into the Rover and switched on the transceiver. I hit the middle of a message:

'. . . Seaside, going east on the A259.'

'Foxtrot Two, was that a positive sighting?'

'A beige Sierra estate with solo driver.'

'You didn't get the registration?'

'No, he passed me as I was making a turn into Whitley Road.'

'Thank you, Foxtrot Two. Out.'

Eastbourne, and heading for Pevensey. But then at once a voice that I recognised as Ringmer's calling in to control.

'Downside Leader. I'm at Ditchling Beacon. Any further sighting from Foxtrot Three?'

But there wasn't, and Ditchling Beacon was going the other way entirely.

'Downside Leader, we have a sighting from Uck-field . . .'

I switched off. I'd heard enough. Nothing positive yet, and long odds that Caudry had gone to earth after making his call. I went on up, to find Gabrielle unpacking the hotel's picnic basket.

'Caudry didn't call back?'

'The shopkeeper, no. But a very nice gentleman, asking for you.'

'Who?'

'He left this number, asking you to call him the moment you returned.'

I knew the number, and dialled it. The phone was picked up at the second ring.

'Gently?'

'Sir.'

'Listen, Gently, what the devil sort of games are you playing in Leyhurst . . .?'

From under his beeches, the A.C. (Crime).

'I've had this tinkle from Whitehall, and this time you *do* stay out of Empton's hair. Good grief man, this business has angles, and you're only there for your own damned amusement. What's it about – do you know this Caudry?'

'He appealed to me for protection.'

'Well, it's gone a damned sight further now, and the message is that you lay off. That clear?'

'I had it from Empton – '

'And now you're getting it from me.'

'Unfortunately, it isn't quite so simple – '

'Nor was the tinkle from the F.O.'

But he listened at last; I gave him a run-down, stressing the dubious nature of Caudry's intelligence. I stressed also, and more particularly, that we had him lined up for two homicides: I knew my man.

'Let's get this straight, Gently. You say we've got him on both counts?'

'One he confessed to me over the phone. On the other we have open-and-shut evidence.'

'Then he belongs to us.'

'To East Sussex.'

'You know what I mean! The F.O. can whistle. At the same time you've got no business there. Damn it man, you're unofficial.'

'Perhaps a word with the C.C.. . .?'

'I don't fancy it, Gently. He'll have had a blast from the F.O. too. But I see your point. If Empton snaffles Caudry, that's likely the last we'll hear of him. And damn it, he's ours. You're sure of that?'

'I think he's close to a full confession.'

'And you've got a line to him?'

'He's got one to me. So far, it's been the only contact.'

The A.C. hummed and ha'd.

'Look, we'll need a *fait accompli*, a written confession to lay on the table. If you think you can get that . . . hmn, don't see why you shouldn't hang about. I don't take kindly to the F.O. telling us what we can and can't do.'

'I'll stay as clear of Empton as I can.'

'Fellow probably on a fool's errand, anyway. But try to keep your nose clean, Gently. And I'd be happier to see you at conference in the morning.'

'And . . . the C.C., sir?'

'Decent chap. Got a daughter who goes eventing with Phyllis.'

I hung up slowly, and reached for a sandwich. At least the godly were seeing it my way! But the A.C. had put his finger on it: we had dire need of that written confession. Gabrielle handed me coffee.

'That was the boss on the line, yes?'

'That was the boss.'

'And you have dealt with this Empton?'

'Perhaps. Only Empton doesn't play by the rules.'

'So still we must get to the shopkeeper first, before Empton and the comrades, perhaps even the good Ringmer?'

'Something like that.'

164

'Then the fool had better ring. Or his fate shall be on his own head.'

But the fool might be finding it difficult to ring, surrounded by Foxtrots and Downside Leaders. Clearly every visit to a call-box was perilous, and patrols might be sitting on his very doorstep. And Empton . . .? He wouldn't cruise for ever, pinning his faith on nebulous sightings. Probably shaping in his mind already was the sort of coverts they'd do well to be drawing. I ate and drank mechanically, willing the silent phone to ring: the sands were running out. In the end, I could not but give Ringmer a hint. Gabrielle said:

'You are thinking grave thoughts, and I am thinking such thoughts also. Since, what can be the end for that frightened man, whose guilt so many will never let die? At the best he must languish in prison, where yet the comrades may reach him, and at worst fall into the hands of your Empton, who may help the comrades to their prey. After all, would it not be merciful for the police to go in with their guns?'

'He is a human being.'

'*Ah oui.* But I am French and feel the shame. Some way out I have been seeking that will make these odds even.'

'Shooting Caudry doesn't solve it.'

'For my life I see no other way. Better that than that the comrades wreak their miserable revenge.'

'He'll be held in a high-security prison.'

'Still, he will live out his life in fear.'

'He would settle for that.'

She sighed. 'And I must not play God, you are saying.'

I said: 'Would you pull the trigger?'

She shook her head. 'No. But, my friend, it is so ignoble. Either that this man lives or that he dies.'

'Perhaps that's what it is to be a traitor.'

'Almost, I am hoping he does not ring.'

We finished our lunch. Outside, the white Renault waited, patient as a stone. Cars passed, time passed,

165

and shadows in the street grew a little longer. In the end I went down to the Rover again to glean what intelligence I might, but Downside Leader had gone to sleep and the Foxtrots had wearied of beige Sierras. Already too late? I was still listening-out when Gabrielle came rushing down the stairs. I was out of the Rover at once.

'It's him?'

'*Oui*. And he sounds quite crazy.'

'Shoot me, monsieur, shoot me! Only, do not let me know when it shall happen.'

'Caudry – pull yourself together!'

'I cannot do it for myself!'

'Stop acting the fool.'

'I have seen them, monsieur, twice now they have passed by. And in the car they have a rope, a new rope – a coil, a bundle of new rope.'

'Who are you talking about?'

'The comrades! Twice they have passed through the village.'

'Four men in a blue Citroen BX?'

'With a rope, monsieur – with a rope!'

'Have they located you?'

'How long can it be?'

'But, as yet, they don't know where you are?'

'They will discover – I must have protection! Monsieur, you cannot leave me to their mercy.'

'Have you also seen the police?'

'I do not care about the police! They will be shooting me too, yes? Protection, monsieur, I must have protection. It is protection that you have promised me.'

In the background, the same hint of surf: and a murmur that may have been a car passing close.

'So tell me where I can find you, Caudry.'

'Oh yes, and then you send in the guns!'

'Unless I know where you are I can't help you.'

166

He made a whining sound. 'I cannot trust you. Except to shoot me, perhaps you do that. It is to be in the back of the neck, monsieur, that is painless, I have seen it done. But I must not know! Promise I shall not. The gun, I shall never see that. In some way you come behind me, place the gun close, fire.'

'Stop talking nonsense!'

'It is painless, monsieur. At once they fall forwards, quite dead. And we can be talking, yes? Then you go to fetch something, and, coming back, when I do not see you – '

'There'll be nothing of that sort.'

'Be merciful, monsieur!'

'You already know my terms.'

'Then I am a doomed man, monsieur. But please, do not let them use the rope!'

Was there any sense left in him? I could hear the ragged, panicky breathing. The coin ran out, and for a moment I thought I was going to lose him. At last the scuffle, the click, the clang, the sound of him juggling with the receiver.

'Caudry?'

An answering whine.

'Now stop this foolishness, and listen. You can trust me, understand? And I'm going to show you that I can trust you. I shall come alone and unarmed. The only gun will be in you hands. I'm going to trust you to put it down and to accept arrest from me. Is that getting through?'

'But then you will shoot me!'

'You can throw the gun into the sea. But somehow you're going to have to trust me, or you're a dead man, Caudry.'

Was the breathing getting slower?

'It is the deal – as before?'

'The same deal. I shall arrest you and be answerable for your security. You will be taken to Leyhurst police station and afterwards lodged in a place of safety. In return you

167

will give a written confession of the killings of Cartier and Bernay.'

The breathing faster!

'But I confess nothing. To save my life is all I do . . .'

'You killed those men.'

'I do not confess! They are men who wish to kill me.'

'Caudry, it's confess or die.'

'You are like the rest, like the Gestapo. And you will come only to shoot me, all is a lie that you say.'

I said: 'Then listen to this, Caudry. You killed an officer of the French Intelligence. That's brought our own intelligence in, and a man quite as cynical as Cartier. I've talked to him. I know his plans. He wants the same information. And when he's got it, he means to hand you over to let the comrades do his dirty work for him. That confession can save you from him, and perhaps is the only thing that will.'

'You lie!'

'Oh no.'

'Yes!'

'That information brought Cartier. Now it's brought another man. And he's out there hunting you now.'

The whining sound; prolonged.

'Monsieur . . . how can I tell?'

'I'm a chance, Caudry. You'll have to take me. Because I'm the only chance you've got.'

'It is self-defence – all.'

'When you killed Bernay?'

'When . . . yes.'

'When you killed Cartier.'

'Both. Both! Did not everyone refuse me protection?'

'Then that you may write in your confession.'

'Still I think you mean to kill me.'

'And I think we understand each other.'

'I cannot tell. I cannot tell.'

The damned coin ran out again, but now the fumbling came quickly: along with the click, the clang, whinings, and another car passing close.

168

'Monsieur!'

'Yes!'

'It shall be . . . as you say. On monsieur's mercy I cast my life. Only, monsieur, come very soon, for I fear even now it is too late.'

'So where do I come?'

'Here, monsieur, here. To a small village by the name of Street. It is by the sea and some miles from Hastings. Monsieur must look for it on a map.'

'And when I get there?'

'A lane to the cliffs, a winding lane through tall bushes. From but a short distance through the village. The cliff is named Furzey Cliff.'

'And at the end of the lane?'

A little whine.

'All alone, this bungalow, monsieur. Because soon it is falling over the cliff, I am able to buy it very cheaply.'

'The name?'

'It is called High Nook, a property derelict and over-grown. There I shall wait your arrival, monsieur. But come very soon. And do not fear the gun.'

The phone clicked dead. Gabrielle was gazing.

'My dear, you would go to that place alone?'

'That's the deal.'

She shook her head firmly. 'We go together, or not at all.'

'Too dangerous.'

'Aha. Too dangerous for me, too dangerous for you. Also, I am thinking you will need another witness when the shopkeeper signs his confession.'

'That can be done later, at the police station.'

'Oh, my friend! And if your Empton is waiting there to grab him? No, no. I come too. It is a French traitor we go to arrest.'

I stared back at her. 'Then, a promise. You will remain in the car.'

'Ha?'

'You will wait in the car while I go in and take his gun.'

169

'That is not fair!'

'But – a promise?'

'Then I promise like a good girl. But come, we waste time, and what is happening we do not know.'

I didn't like it, but I went along. While she opened the gates, I explored the map. Street was a hamlet of one or two houses in a tangle of minor roads, but if there was such a lane and such a bungalow it found no credit with the map. I drove out. We locked the gates. I edged the Rover up to the junction. All under the eyes of the white Renault, from whose exhaust came a puff of smoke.

12

But dropping the Renault was a minor problem, calling for mere sleight of hand. From Ringmer's office I had observed a rear exit to the M.T. yard behind the police station. I coasted the Rover thither, with the Renault trailing behind, turned in at the entrance and there paused, watching events in my mirror. At once the Renault pulled in to the kerb, halting with full view of the station; the brother was driving, and in the back I recognised the newcomer who'd arrived that morning. I let the Rover coast again, slowly, as though I were looking for a slot to park, until we were out of sight of the Renault and heading for that convenient exit. At which point Malling came running from the building, waving as he came. I paused and dropped my window.

'Sir! The C.C. was on the phone. Says to tell you that, as from now, you have full official status.'

Well; that was nice to know.

'So give me the official situation.'

'Chiefy is patrolling out Bexhill way, sir. They had a possible sighting from Henley's Down. There's also one in from Penhurst. It's all in the same area.'

'Is Chief Super Empton with him?'

'No sir. He split off towards the coast.'

Yes indeed.

'I'll be listening out. Keep all movements coming over the air.'

I quit the yard, began driving. So Empton was sniffing the air already. And where else would his nostrils take him but to the bungalow-enclaves that infested the coast? There, strangers were the norm, not to mention Ford estates; a man looking for a bolt-hole could probably choose no better. And Bexhill was next-door to Hastings: how long before Empton smelled out High Nook?

'You are worried, yes?'

'I am worried.'

'Yet, this bungalow must be well-concealed.'

'That's just what makes it vulnerable to Empton. He'll be on the look out for such places.'

'Still, he must first find it, and there are many places to seek. I think he will not be there so soon. And over the radio he is hearing these things.'

'These things' were a call-in from Brighton, where a Frenchman had been detained on the Front, and another from Pevensey Bay, one more sighting of one more Ford.

'He'll listen. But he won't be fooled.'

'Yet we know these are idle. And he does not.'

I hoped she was right but didn't bank on it: smarter than Empton ferrets didn't come.

I hit the A27, cursing the Sunday trippers who littered it, skirted Eastbourne and set course through Pevensey to Bexhill. I should have noticed, but I didn't, a car that was waiting at a sideroad junction; just a car, until an exclamation from Gabrielle told me different.

'My dear – look in your mirror!'

I looked, and swore: the blue Citroen. It was sitting directly on my tail, the faces of its crew intent on the Rover.

'What shall we do?'

'We'll have to ditch them.'

No doubt that they recognised our car. I accelerated, overtook, and still the Citroen was sitting there. Pranks in Bexhill? I thought better of it, saw a minor road signed ahead, braked at the last possible moment and made a howling turn into it.

'They have gone past!'

They hadn't any option! But how long before they were back? And their presence here suggested another thing: that they were pursuing the same course as Empton. I scoured down that minor road, which seemed to lead only into darkest Sussex, but brought me suddenly to a main-road junction where traffic was going past in a queue.

'My dear, I can see them!'

So could I, as I went for a gap that was barely there. Then, another sideroad, hard right at a fork, and back to the road I'd first thought of.

'We lose them, I think.'

But just to be certain I took the next sideroad, an unsigned track. Finally I slowed my pace to a crawl and inspected the mirror. We were alone. I pulled on to a verge.

'Hand me the map.'

The time had come for a low profile. Not only the Citroen was combing the coast roads, checking out the area bit by bit. Main roads, the towns were out; I traced a course on untinted ways. A couple of A-roads must needs be crossed but otherwise it should be just us and Sussex. I handed back the map.

'Keep it open. Signposts may be far to seek.'

'It is not far now?'

'Not far. Provided we hit no more snags.'

Fast I could not drive along those winding, rambling lanes, leading one into another, past straw-thatch cottages and distant farms. They kept the high ground: across the fields appeared the urbations we were evading and, at last, the grey sea, slowly swinging round towards us. Came to our last A-road: no glimpse of Citroen, glimpse of Jaguar. We crossed it; entered a road signed with the single name: Street.

'We are close, ha?'

'Close.'

Another two miles found us the village. It lay low, facing a beach on which a couple of longshore boats were pulled up. Just a few houses. Not even a pub. And at once the road was rising again, clambering up heathy, bushy heights that cut off sharply towards the sea.

'See – there!'

A weathered phone-box, standing neighbour to the hut of a fisherman; well up the road from the houses, and overshadowed by heather slopes.

'From there he rings, yes?'

And he could probably reach it without using the road; the ghost of a path ran through the heather, vanishing soon among green gorses.

'Just remember your promise.'

'Aha.'

I drove on, out of sight of the houses. The road levelled, began to open a view of the low shore towards Dungeness. And I nearly missed it: a stony track taking off through the gorses, winding upwards towards a summit where grew a few stunted birches. I backed, turned in, drove at walking pace. The track was longer than appeared. But at last it emerged in an open space. Where a timber bungalow stood at the very cliff-edge.

'This will do.'

I'd put anchors down at once, while we were still fifty yards from the bungalow. Nothing had moved up there, though the front door was hanging ajar. A decrepit-looking structure shedding chalky-green paint, patches of felt gone from the roof, greyed curtains at dirty windows: the final refuge of Caudry/Darlan. Looking out to sea. To France. Trouville.

I got slowly from the car, then slammed the door and stood quite still. The beige estate was parked in the gorse, just its bonnet poking out. The open space had been once a garden, now was overgrown with rank grass and brambles. Through the sagging door one looked through the building to other dirty windows, behind them sky.

'Caudry!'

No answer.

'Caudry – show yourself!'

He didn't. No movement, no sound, except the dulled murmur of the surf.

'I'm coming in, Caudry.'

I held out my hands and began walking deliberately towards the bungalow. Now from the corner of my eye I could see the estate, but the estate appeared empty. I stumbled over remains of crazy-paving, halted a yard or two from the door, listened intently, heard nothing, took another step forward.

'Caudry! Stop playing games. I'm coming in, you understand?'

Then I heard it: a faint movement in the gorses on my left.

'Stay very still, monsieur.'

Very slowly indeed, I turned. He had come out from behind a bush, gun in hand, the gun pointing at my navel. I said:

'Give it me.'

He was crouching, grimacing, an idiot-grin on his hollow-cheeked face.

'I am the boss, monsieur, yes?'

'Just hand it over. We haven't time for comedy.'

'But I am still the boss, ha?'

'Caudry, if you keep this up, you're dead.'

'And if I do not, dead too, monsieur? I think you do not come here as you say. You shall be alone, that is the deal, and I see another in the car.'

'Madame my wife. As you very well know.'

'But why, monsieur? It is not the deal.'

'She is here to help save your miserable life. To witness your signature on the confession.'

He made the whining noise. 'And I am believing this? Monsieur, it is not as you say.'

'Oh, for God's sake, pull yourself together, Caudry!'

'Monsieur, I have the gun. I still have the gun.'

175

It wasn't heroism, just pure irritation: I walked straight up to him and held out my hand. And like a detached observer I was seeing the mortal fear in his staring eyes.

'Give.'

He whined and chattered, a wreck of a being, scarcely human: then shoved the gun into my hands and fell on his knees among the gorses.

'From behind, monsieur, in the neck. Oh please, quickly. Oh please!'

'Get up, you lunatic!'

'In the neck. In the neck. Quickly, monsieur – please, quickly!'

I grabbed him and yanked him bawling to his feet.

'Not this way, monsieur – no, no!'

There was no help for it, I slapped the lank cheeks, blows that must have rattled his brain. He fell back sobbing, clutching his face, his eyes still bolting with terror.

'Don't – don't. Shoot me now!'

I slipped the magazine out of the gun, emptied the shells into my hand, flung them piecemeal into the gorses. Then I pocketed the gun and stared at Caudry.

'You have another gun – the lady is bringing it!'

I felt like kicking him. 'You've had your fun. Now get inside there and start scribbling.'

'I confess, and then you shoot me?'

'You confess, and I march you into a cell.'

'It will be after that – ?'

'Get inside! And try not to blubber in front of the lady.'

But he couldn't stop himself. Trembling, sobbing, he staggered towards the steps of the bungalow, with Gabrielle, who'd come over when she saw I had the gun, watching all with shocked eyes.

'My dear, he is no longer responsible.'

'That's for the courts to decide.'

'Perhaps he should just be kept in a hospital?'

I shrugged. 'Then it must be one with very high walls.'

Shabby cheap furniture of the 'thirties occupied the room we entered, dark-stained wood, worn rexine, a faded carpet showing the thread. Bleached paper bagged from the walls, stained fibre-board sagged from the ceiling: life had departed from that room many a summer's day since. It had, however, a long bay window, facing directly to the sea. And revealing a six-foot wide strip of grass that ended abruptly in space.

'Monsieur . . . there is here no paper.'

But I'd taken care of that. Sheets of paper taken from the shop with a printed heading that included his name.

'I have no pen . . .'

'Here.'

'I do not know . . .'

'First write the date.'

He was still shaking so much that he had difficulty in getting going.

'I do not admit . . .'

'Keep it simple. We can expand it later on. But if your plea is self-defence there will have to be a reason given.'

'It is that the traitor Bernay would have killed me!'

'I'm afraid you may have to do better than that.'

'No – I cannot!' The pen was bobbing in his hand. 'As much as that I confess. But no more.'

'You will have to explain Cartier.'

'Just that I killed him.'

'Then self-defence goes out of the window. You can't have it both ways, Caudry. Either you're Darlan, or you're a motiveless killer.'

'I cannot. I cannot.'

Gabrielle said: 'It will be best, monsieur. This is a secret which is no more a secret. You will reveal only that you are still a man.'

'Darlan is dead.'

'But that man you were. This is all that Monsieur Caudry must say.'

He stared at her, huge-eyed. Then whimpered pitifully.

'No. I cannot!'

'Then, already too late.'

He would have jumped up from the little deal table where I had sat him down to write, but I pushed him back in the chair, held him down by his shoulders.

'Just write.'

In the end, I had to dictate every word. No mention of motive: a simple confession of crimes, times and places. Given under duress? That was for the courts, and meanwhile I had Cartier's gun in my pocket. For the moment, the confession was all, and Whitehall, Empton, could go whistle.

'Sign it.'

He grimaced idiotically.

'You have not kept back . . . the one bullet?'

'Sign it!'

'But then, perhaps . . .?'

He winced at my glare, shakily scribbled his signature. I added mine. Gabrielle hers. I folded the sheet and tucked it away.

'Right. You are under arrest, Caudry, and you will accompany me to the police station. There will be formally charged, and detained in secure custody.'

'But the deal, monsieur – the deal!'

'After interrogation you may talk to your lawyer.'

'After interrogation . . .?'

'We shall require in detail what you have given in brief here.'

'But . . . interrogation?'

'Just get to the car!'

He sprang up. 'Monsieur has deceived me – no inter-rogation! This is not part of the deal, monsieur, it is better for me that you use the gun.'

'Get to the car!'

'No!'

'Monsieur,' Gabrielle said.'This is a misunderstanding. The English police do not torture their prisoners, it is a simple matter of question and answer.'

'Ha, no. I am not trusting, of these things I know very well.'

'You are in grave error, monsieur. No harm whatever is intended to yourself.'

She may have convinced him, may not; but at that instant the matter became academic. Reached us the sound of an approaching engine, and all our eyes switched to the track. A car appeared. The Citroen. It crept up beside the Rover, and there parked.

'Shoot me. Shoot me. In mercy, shoot me!'

The four had alighted from the car: Brezolles, Nogent, Dreux and Houdan, the pork-butcher carrying a coil of new rope.

'I will jump over the cliff – yes!'

They'd advanced to the crazy-paving, and stopped. Stood now, shoulder to shoulder, gazing empty-faced, silent.

'I am deceived. This was all planned. You have my confession, and now – !'

'Stay put, Caudry.'

'Yes, aha, you will leave me now, because you do not wish to see!'

'Stay where you are.'

'I am betrayed!'

He was shaking too much to attempt an escape: the gaunt face transfigured, eyes glazed in a crazy stare.

'Stay here while I talk to them.'

179

'You do not shoot me – aha, now I see! A bullet you have to explain, yes? But not this way – no, no!'

Gabrielle said: 'Courage, monsieur. You are a prisoner of the police.'

'I am betrayed – I am betrayed! In this world, not one to trust.'

Brezolles had stepped forward; the encounter could no longer be delayed. I shoved Caudry on a settee, where he'd be out of sight, and went down the rotten steps of that wretched bungalow. I confronted Brezolles.

'Monsieur.'

'Monsieur.'

'What purpose brings you here, monsieur?'

'Monsieur, we have private business which it is meet that we carry out. It concerns but us, monsieur, and I observe your car parked by our own. I suggest, monsieur, that, with madame your wife, you leave us to proceed as our conscience prompts.'

'I cannot leave without my prisoner, monsieur.'

'I am desolate, monsieur, but he must stay with us.'

'He is under arrest for serious crimes.'

'No more so, monsieur, than those for which we bring justice.'

'Monsieur, I must point out that we are in England, and that I represent the legal authority.'

'Monsieur, against my will, you force me also to point out that we are four, and you are one.'

'You would proceed by force?'

'With intense regret.'

'Your punishment will be severe, monsieur.'

'That shall be as God wills.'

'The will of the court will be imprisonment for life.' I looked around at the other three stony faces. 'Messieurs, this applies to all,' I said. 'Should you continue in this criminal exploit, the English courts will show no mercy. You may expect each a sentence of twenty years. Some of you will never see France again. Those who do will

180

be old men. I advise you strongly to give up your intentions.'

They looked at me, but none spoke.

'Monsieur,' Brezolles said. 'We have heard you out. Now, in short, you must hear us. We bring to England the justice of France for the betrayal and murder of brave men. The blood of the martyrs of Trouville cries out for that justice to be done. In France, this is understood. In England, it must be as it may. But, at last, the traitor is run to earth, and his shame is ours if we fail in our purpose.'

'Your shame – your shame!'

I was pushed aside: now it was Gabrielle who confronted Brezolles.

'Monsieur – messieurs – it is shame that I feel, to hear Frenchmen speak so to my English husband! Your shame is not that you let Darlan live, but that you are here at all, messieurs – that still, one whole forty years on, you have not cast off such delusions as these. Are you men, or are you underworld creatures, things without heart and even without brain? What evil is driving you to commit this crime, in the name of a justice that cannot be upheld?'

'Madame, you are French, you should better understand – '

'Monsieur, not only am I French. I am the daughter of Jacques Orbec, the leader of the comrades in Rouen. And I ask you, what do you do? What delusions are you still pursuing? I find you seeking the life of a man, who, for so long, has been an honest citizen, and would have been so yet were it not for the like of yourselves.'

'He is Darlan – '

'Darlan is dead!'

'Madame, we know him to be in that dwelling.'

'In that dwelling, monsieur, is Jean Caudry, a respectable shopkeeper from a nearby town.'

'Darlan!'

'Jean Caudry. Who was born on the day that Darlan died. Who since then has sold his tents and his sheepskins, with never a question against his name. You are seeking a ghost, monsieur, the ghost of a man who once was. And you have driven this honest shopkeeper to crimes for which he must answer. But not to you.'

'Madame, this is sophistry!'

'Aha. And what say the rest of you, messieurs?'

The rest of them were looking uncomfortable, especially the pork-butcher with his coil of rope.

'You do not answer me, messieurs. Can it be, at last, that you feel ashamed – that a little light begins to dawn on the long night of your delusions? Don't be afraid! The shopkeeper has confessed. The English law will take its course. To Evreux you may return with the tidings that Bernay has been avenged. But not if you pursue your criminal ends to the shame of myself and to that of France. So, what say you?'

Brezolles said desperately: 'It is no matter! We come for a traitor.'

'Then you must seek him in Trouville, monsieur, because, here, we have only the shopkeeper.'

'I repeat, you speak sophistry!'

Gabrielle said: 'Yet monsieur the pork-butcher is putting down his rope. And monsieur the builder is looking unhappy, while monsieur the clerk is studying his shoes.'

Dreux muttered: 'We can talk, Bertrand.'

'Lucien, the time for talking is over!'

'There is logic in what she says.'

'Still will you listen to the tongue of a woman?'

'I say we talk.'

'I say no!'

But already Dreux was turning away, to be followed by Nogent and Houdan; the reluctant Brezolles was obliged to join them. Gabrielle was hot-faced and breathing fast.

'We have not won the day yet, my friend.'

'Where is Caudry?'

'I left him on the settee, with his hands pressed to his ears.'

I cast a look towards the bungalow: no sound, no movement in that direction. But only the cliff-edge lay behind. Caudry could jump, but he couldn't escape.

'Here they come.'

And now it was Dreux who was leading the little group, with Brezolles, sulky-looking, trailing in the rear. Dreux faced us.

'Monsieur. Madame.'

'Monsieur.'

'Monsieur, we have come to this decision. We shall do no harm to that man there, but see him we must. On this we insist.'

'You will do him no harm?'

'Monsieur.'

I touched the coil of rope with my foot.

'In that case, you won't need this. And I require that you dump it over that cliff.'

Just a moment of silence; then Dreux stooped, picked up the rope and marched to the cliff-edge. We saw the coil whirled above his head and cast into space. Dreux marched back.

'Now, monsieur.'

'Remain here. I will inform him of your intention.'

'Wait,' Gabrielle said. 'Messieurs, your word upon the cross that you will not harm him.'

A longer silence! Finally, led by Dreux, each crossed himself: and the cross they sketched on their breasts was the doubled cross of Lorraine.

I turned, strode back to the bungalow, up the rotten steps, through the door. Caudry was where I had left him, sprawled on the rexine-covered settee. But, not as I had left him. His face was contorted, eyes fixed in a stare, knees dragged to his stomach. And there was foam on his grinning lips.

'Caudry!'

183

The stare didn't change.

'Caudry – what have you done?'

In his throat, a sort of convulsion; then he gasped:

'. . . it works . . .!'

I threw myself down by the settee. What I was smelling was a faint odour of almonds.

He was still alive when they filed in, but his eyes rolled a moment later. Brezolles it was who stooped to sniff, then nod to his empty-faced companions.

'*La pilule du Gestapo. C'est à propos – justice est faite.*'

He spat on Caudry. Houdan spat. Nogent spat. Dreux didn't spit. He remained longest staring down at the convulsed body on the shabby settee, and, as he turned away, murmured almost inaudibly:

'*Le pauvre bâtard!*'

Gabrielle, white-faced, muttered to me:

'No problem, my friend. No problem now.'

And perhaps she was right. There was only this way. The body on the settee and the smell of almonds.

'All is one.'

Caudry/Darlan. Knitted in an instant by sparkling cyanide.

But the time for moralising was brief; another car had arrived up the track. Swearing as he tripped on the rotten steps, Empton came storming into the bungalow. He stared at the scene with savage eyes.

'You sod – you've let the frogs get at him!'

'I didn't have to,' I said. 'He got at himself.'

'You'll answer for it – oh yes, you'll answer! You knew where he was, and I didn't get told.'

'Because you weren't on the case.'

'Sonny-boy!'

'Not on the case,' I said. 'Caudry was wanted for double murder. He belonged to the Sussex Police.'

'Your feet won't touch.'

'I have his signed confession.'

184

'And you were warned to stay clear, sunbeam!'

'Ask around,' I said. 'Things change. This looks like Ringmer turning up now.'

He made to strike me. He didn't manage it. Dreux had been watching this short exchange. As Empton picked himself up from the lino, Dreux, who hadn't spat on Caudry, spat on Empton.

Then Ringmer arrived, wide-eyed, and it was time to get down to business.

I wrote my report in Ringmer's office, and after that we didn't linger. The unlit shop across the street from The Swinburne was a neighbour that neither of us felt able to live with. In the little lounge I noticed a solemn celebration, in which, however, a champagne-bucket figured; in passing, I caught the eye of Madame Bernay, and she made a gesture. But I shook my head.

'Damn it, I wanted to shake your hand, Gently – introduce you to the lady wife.'

Only that was on the phone and easily fielded; we booked out of The Swinburne as they were serving dinner.

Empton, I knew, had preceded me to town, and by now my name would be mud in Whitehall. Perhaps I should have been concerned about that, but, somehow I wasn't feeling able to manage it. We drove on into the suburbs before stopping for a meal; and that, too, was a sorry affair, bearing only a rueful resemblance to food.

'My dear, I am feeling one thousand years old.'

Gabrielle had been silent till now. All the way from Leyhurst her hand had lain inert on my knee. On an impulse, I said:

'Let's just keep on driving.'

'Ha . . .?'

'We can be at Heatherings before midnight.'

'Oh, my dear!'

And suddenly that was an answer, lit a spark of light in our gloom.

'We shall not be expected.'

'We can phone.'

'Are you not required for work in the morning?'

'So I'll take a day off.'

'I think you are naughty!'

'Put it down to sea air.'

So we did that, we kept on driving, in a night that was starlit when we'd left the town behind: the night of the Sunday after the storm, when the roads to our home were clear again. Down there the Channel, down there the cliff-top, down there a scene that rode with us still. But Heatherings ahead. And, before we arrived, Gabrielle had fallen sound asleep.

The next morning a chain-saw was moaning over the wreck of our copper beech, and we were sadly viewing the overturned shrubs, the collapsed fences, the shattered greenhouse. It took a fortnight to clear it up, till we could see the change we must learn to live with; but at least the house had taken small harm, and the Walks still beckoned through the garden gate. And, a fortnight later, a little event.

'The postman brings me a package, my dear. It is not from Rouen, but from Honfleur, and the handwriting that of the good Frenaye.'

'From Frenaye . . .?'

'But yes. See. It contains a letter, and this small, sealed, box.'

We read the letter together. 'My very dear Madame,' Frenaye had written. 'I return recently from Evreux, where I am visiting my mother. While there I am approached by the four gentlemen who had lately the pleasure of your acquaintance in England, and, from them, I have intelligence of the miserable end of the traitor, Darlan. For you, madame, they express great admiration, and wish you to accept the enclosed token, which, to avoid revealing your postal directions, I undertook to convey myself. To their admiration may I add my own, and compliments to yourself and to Monsieur George.'

We examined the box.

'It is not a bomb, ha?'

'I don't think it can be a bomb.'

Something small rattled inside: I broke the seal and opened the box. What it contained was a silver Cross of Lorraine on a silver chain, and a card inscribed: For a true Daughter of France/From the Patriots of Evreux.

Poor Gabrielle blushed crimson. 'The fools. They are chauvinists to the end!'

'But you'll wear it, won't you?'

'We shall see.'

It appeared, very shyly, at our friend Capel's next musical evening.

Brundall, 1987/88